THE WOODEN TOKENS

DAWN KNOX

British Library Cataloguing in Publication Data A Record of this Publication is available from the British Library

ISBN: 9798378855384

Formatting and Cover © Paul Burridge at www.publishingbuddy.co.uk
Editing – Wendy Ogilvie Editorial Services

To my mum, Amelia May, after whom I named the ship, the Lady Amelia. And to my dad.

Thank you both for believing in me.

CHAPTER 1

1768:

Two babies. One girl, one boy.

Side-by-side in adjacent cots, they seemed to gurgle and chortle at each other.

"Piffle!" the senior nurse in the ward said when one of her less experienced charges had suggested such a thing. Although she had conceded it was a blessing they weren't howling like the six other babies who'd been admitted to the Foundling Hospital that day.

A piece of paper bearing the letter 'G' was pinned to the girl's fine, silk shawl while the letter attached to the boy's coarse, woollen blanket was 'H'. They'd been left in the hospital within half an hour of each other and had been registered one after the other.

Two mothers – both called Margaret – each in such a desperate situation, she felt the only option was to give her baby up to the Foundling Hospital. Neither mother would ever see her child again.

Earlier, a coach bearing the livery of the Duke of Westervale had stopped some way from Lamb's Conduit Field, Bloomsbury, London, and a respectably dressed, middle-aged woman alighted carrying a baby. Muffled sobs escaped from the coach and the curtain jerked aside, revealing a young red-headed woman who pressed her palms to the glass as if to reach out to pull the infant back. Mrs Barrett, the housekeeper who bore the baby away dared not look back at her beloved mistress for fear she'd be unable to carry on with what must be done.

Lady Margaret Farringdon, daughter and only child of the Duke of Westervale had spent most of the year with her aunt in Brighton, taking the sea air. Few knew that during that time, she'd given birth to a daughter, Caroline Farringdon, who now lay placidly in the housekeeper's arms.

The Duke was unaware of his illegitimate granddaughter. He spent much of his time with his parliamentary friends and had not remarked on his daughter's extended stay with his deceased wife's sister by the seaside.

Mrs Barrett looked down at the auburn-haired baby and her heart constricted. How she longed to keep the child herself. She and her mistress had discussed the baby's future, they'd exhausted every possibility, and had both concluded there was no alternative. Lady

Margaret had sent one hundred pounds with a letter to the Foundling Hospital begging them to take Caroline and they'd agreed. Surely, the child had a better chance at the hospital than anywhere else? They had an impressive reputation for care. The wealthiest and most influential patrons and the finest nurses and doctors. And they were discreet. What more could one ask?

After Caroline had been inspected by the doctor, a nurse carried her into the office where Mrs Barrett was waiting on the edge of her chair. If the baby was found to be carrying any infectious diseases, might she be rejected? Then what would Lady Margaret do? But the nurse had nodded and smiled at the secretary.

"The babe is well."

The man at the desk took a fresh billet from his drawer and after dipping his pen in the ink, he wrote 'G', the child's letter, at the top. After he'd taken note of Caroline's clothes and fine silk blanket, a small square of fabric was cut from her blue and white gown near the hem, including the white ribbon trim. The square was cut in two and one of the pieces was pinned to the billet. Then he duplicated the form and pinned the other piece of blue and white cloth to that.

"Do you have a token?" He looked up at Mrs Barrett and smiled kindly.

She withdrew a pair of emerald earrings and handed them to him.

He pushed one back towards her. "We keep one and the mother retains the other. In that way, if she wants to reclaim her daughter in the future, we can all be certain that the correct child is returned to her. She will need to supply us with the identifying letter and today's date. We'll match everything up and the child will be returned to her."

When he'd finished, he satisfied himself the ink was dry, then he sealed the token inside the folded billet with wax and after unlocking a container, he placed it inside.

Mrs Barrett had been so intent on watching the man seal the billet and deposit it in the box, she didn't notice the nurse slip away with baby Caroline. When she looked up and saw they'd gone, pain, once again crushed her heart. She thought of her mistress outside in the carriage sobbing piteously. If Mrs Barrett felt so wretched, what agonies must Lady Margaret be experiencing?

"It's for the best," the secretary said, nodding towards where the nurse and baby had been seconds before.

Mrs Barrett inclined her head. She couldn't reply for the lump in her throat. He was probably right. He must have witnessed this scene many times before. It was best she hadn't seen the child go.

He coughed gently and looked at her expectantly. Of course, he had other women to interview. Other babies to record. Mrs Barrett rose and left the office, dreading the thought of describing what had just taken place to her distraught mistress.

They must both put this behind them.

Lady Margaret would have to return to her old life as if nothing had changed. Her father had suggested several suitors and would expect her to marry before the end of the year. An illegitimate child would have ruined everything. But now, the slate had been wiped clean. She would be able to start a new family. It wouldn't be easy, but it was Lady Margaret's duty and Mrs Barrett knew she understood that.

However, Lady Margaret didn't live long enough for her father to arrange a suitable match. After the clandestine trip to Bloomsbury, she lost her appetite and experienced severe insomnia. Eventually, she took to her bed. At first, her father suggested another trip to stay with her aunt in Brighton, and he was baffled by her vehement rejection of his idea. Hadn't she written on several occasions over the last year to tell him how much she enjoyed Brighton and its healthy sea air?

He summoned the family physician who bled her repeatedly.

"Melancholia and hysteria," the physician pronounced with a roll of his eyes towards the ceiling as if he considered her condition simply a deplorable lack of effort on her part.

Lady Margaret became weaker until she no longer had the stamina to rise at all.

Eventually, the Duke dismissed the physician whose attempts to balance her humours by bloodletting seemed to be making her worse and left her to the care of trusty Mrs Barrett, the housekeeper. Gradually, Lady Margaret's health declined until one night, clutching a small piece of fabric that the Duke didn't recognise and one of her emerald earrings, she slipped away. His beautiful daughter. Aged twenty-two, with so much life still before her. An inexplicable tragedy.

The dark-haired boy's beginnings were humbler than those of the aristocratic girl in the adjacent cradle. He'd been born to Joseph Wright, a sailor, and his wife, Margaret. The union had been loving but brief because three days after they'd become man and wife, Joseph had returned to his ship and sailed to the East Indies. News of the great storm that resulted in the loss of his ship and all hands reached Margaret almost nine months later. The shock hastened the birth of their son who was born the following day. A healthy baby boy whom she called Joseph after his father.

After the dreadful news and the complicated birth of her son, Margaret failed to recover her strength. Perhaps she couldn't bear the insurmountable problems that faced her and the baby. She wouldn't be able to return to her post as maid in the grand house with a child. And her savings wouldn't last. In a month or two, she wouldn't be able to pay the rent nor buy food.

And she felt so desperately ill as if life was draining out of her. She suspected she might not live much longer. If she survived, she must take Joseph to the parish and ask for them both to be admitted to the workhouse. If she died, then who knew what might happen to her baby? There was only one other possibility but for that, she needed help. And to acquire that help, she'd need a lot of luck.

Margaret summoned all her energy and holding young Joseph in her arms she trudged from her cottage to the grand house where she'd once worked. At the servants' entrance, she pleaded to see her former employer's wife.

When she heard about Joseph's tragic death, Lady Chesselford shook her head and clucked her tongue sadly, expecting her former maid to ask for alms. Her handbell was within easy reach to summon a servant to lead the poor woman out, should that be the case. Of course, first, she'd explain that she was a charitable woman and sympathetic to her former maid's plight. Then, she'd send her to the kitchen for some food. But that would be that. Lady Chesselford could hardly be expected to subsidise every past employee who fell on hard times.

However, when she'd heard Margaret's request, she said she wasn't sure Lord Chesselford would be able – or indeed – willing, to do anything. Margaret broke down and begged. Lady Chesselford was moved and agreed to try to persuade her husband. Well, why not? It wouldn't cost her anything and Chesselford was one of the governors of the Foundling Hospital in London. If he couldn't do anything, who could? It wasn't like she was going to offer the woman the one hundred pounds that she understood would ensure the poor, unfortunate child gained a place in the institution.

When Margaret walked home later with Joseph asleep in one arm and a package containing a loaf of bread, cheese and ham cradled in the other, she also had Lady Chesselford's assurances that she'd do all she could to secure a place for Joseph in the Foundling Hospital.

Several days later, Lord Chesselford's coach driver called at Margaret's cottage to give her the good news. Lord Chesselford had testified to his fellow members of the board of governors of Mrs Wright's good character and unhappy circumstances and as a favour to him, a place would be available for young Joseph Wright, on condition that he arrive on the date and time given and that he pass the health checks. Furthermore, Lady Chesselford had arranged for a local farmer to convey mother and child to Bloomsbury on his way to market.

On the given day, Margaret waited until Joseph had been examined by the doctor to ensure he was healthy and didn't carry any infectious diseases. To her enormous relief, he was accepted. The farmer had arranged to take her back to the village that evening but Margaret had other plans. She thanked him and told him she'd decided to stay with her sister overnight. It was a lie, but she was sure God would forgive her. With tears streaming down her face, she walked out of the hospital gate and after asking for directions to the River Thames, she set off. One weary foot in front of the other. Hardly aware of her surroundings or the increasing bustle as she approached the river. The fresh breeze breathed a little life back into her, giving her the strength to descend a set of stone steps down to the water. There was nothing more she could do for her son. And the arms of her beloved husband awaited.

The body of an unknown woman was found three days later washed up on the foreshore at Wapping. A small square of grey cloth was pinned to her bodice.

On Sunday, all the children who'd been left in the care of the Foundling Hospital that week were dressed in new clothes and taken into the chapel in the grounds. Around the neck of each child was a ribbon, attached to which was a round, metal disc stamped with the child's unique identifying number. Each baby was baptised and given a new name – whether they already had one or not.

Caroline Farringdon, child number 16,700 and Joseph Wright, child number 16,701 had both been present in the chapel. By the end of the service, the girl had become Anne Sherrington and the boy had become Benjamin Haywood.

During one week, the babies had lost, not only their mothers but the clothes that each woman had dressed them in and the names they'd chosen for them.

But compared to many thousands of babies who'd been handed over to the workhouse or indeed abandoned on the streets, at least Anne and Benjamin would be well cared for. And to begin with, they'd be well-loved too.

CHAPTER 2

Isabella, wife of James Trent, a prosperous Essex farmer, rocked a cradle with each hand. She gazed with love at the tiny auburn head in one and the dark head in the other. Tears came to her eyes as she remembered her own twin boys who'd died days after their birth. So, to have these two babies was indeed a blessing from God.

Her sister had suggested she apply to the Foundling Hospital for a child to fill a cradle – and her life. At first, she'd been reluctant. Too grief-stricken. But Mr Trent had also suggested it might do her good and eventually, he'd written to the hospital. The board of governors sent an inspector who'd scrutinised the farmhouse and questioned her and Mr Trent. Thanks be to God, he'd been satisfied with them. He'd reported back to the board that in his opinion, she'd be a suitable wet nurse and that she and Mr Trent would be fitting guardians for a child. Then, the startling and wonderful news – two babies would be available, and would she be able to take a second one?

The other child was to have been placed with a wet nurse who'd contracted smallpox during an outbreak and no one else could be found at such short notice. Since Mrs Trent had given birth to twins, perhaps she might be able to take the second child...?

Shortly after, Mr and Mrs Trent travelled to London to pick up Anne Sherrington and Benjamin Haywood. As the babies exchanged hands, the couple was informed that an inspector would visit them regularly to check on the children's welfare and a new set of clothes for each child would be provided once a year.

And now, God willing, Anne and Benjamin would grow up as her children until they were five. That was so far in the future, Isabella didn't feel the need to worry. Anything could happen in five years, and she was determined to enjoy every moment.

Isabella continued to rock the two cradles. Anne opened her eyes and waved her chubby fist in the air, then sucked it. Isabella's heart melted and the breath caught in her throat. Such a beautiful child. No one would call Benjamin beautiful. Dark and intense. But he was no less precious in her eyes.

"My darling, Annie." She picked up the girl and settled back in her chair to feed her. Benjamin would be awake soon. It was as if the two were joined by an invisible cord. When one woke, the other woke shortly after. But that of course was just fanciful nonsense.

1773:

"Annie! Annie! Pull me up!"

Below the tree bough on which she was sitting, Annie's three-year-old brother, Robert, held up his chubby arms towards her. Hanging onto his smock was their younger sister, Sarah, aged two. With her thumb in her mouth, she looked up into the apple tree with huge eyes.

"You're too little to climb the tree, Rob, but I'll bring you and Sarah a lovely apple," Annie said.

Before Rob had a chance to reply, Ben leapt from his hiding place and swept the little boy up in his arms. Rob squealed in delight and even Sarah took her thumb out of her mouth and laughed. Ben was tall and strong for a five-year-old but with plump Rob in his arms, he overbalanced, and the two boys fell over, gasping for breath. They rolled down the hill followed by Sarah. Annie picked four apples and tucking them in her apron, clambered down the trunk to check the boys. It wouldn't do if Rob was hurt. Ma had been rather tearful during the last few weeks and had frequently scolded them all. It was so unlike her.

Even Pa seemed quieter than usual. And although he still allowed the four children to scramble over him like a human mountain, the last time they'd done it, she'd thought she'd seen tears in his eyes and wondered if they were hurting him. But it was hard to tell. Pa never complained and he certainly never cried.

Ma did. She'd been sobbing every so often since a stranger had arrived several weeks before. He'd brought a new set of clothes for her and Ben. Why Ma would find that upsetting, Annie had no idea.

"Me! Me!" Sarah held out her hands to Ben whose arms were around Rob and who was spinning dizzily. The young boy's legs flew outwards, and he squealed in mock terror.

Ben picked up Sarah and swung her around too – only more gently – to her great indignation.

"Fast! Me fast like Robbie!" she yelled, urging him on as they spun like a sycamore seed twirling in the wind. He put her down and staggered dizzily while the others shook with laughter. Annie distributed the apples and they lay on their backs in the grass, watching the clouds scud overheard while they ate the sweet fruit.

Rob grew restless first. "Play beetles!" He jumped to his feet and turned his back to them, his arms out to his sides. Ben rose and with his back to the young boy, they linked arms at the elbow.

"Go, beetle!" Sarah yelled, leaping to her feet.

Ben leaned forwards and swung Rob up onto his back, flinging the small boy's feet up in the air. Putting Rob down and letting go of his arms, he repeated it with Sarah. Annie was almost the same height as Ben and they locked arms, back-to-back, then to the younger children's delight, she leaned forwards and holding tightly onto his arms with hers, she lifted Ben onto her back, flinging his legs upwards. When his feet were back on the ground, he bent forwards, throwing her legs high in the air. Back and forth, one supported the other whilst their partner kicked their legs high.

"Like a beetle waggling its legs!" Sarah cried.

And, indeed, to Annie, it seemed like she and Ben had joined together to form a completely new body.

When they tired, Ben pretended his arms had locked in place and he couldn't release Annie, so they staggered over the grass, back-to-back, while the younger ones shouted encouragement to Annie to slip away or to Ben to keep her trapped.

The afternoon passed in childish games and stomach-aching laughter. Golden sun, lush green grass and apple juice-sticky lips.

It was to be the last afternoon the children ever spent together.

That evening, Ma and Pa were more silent than ever. The grass stains on the children's smocks from the afternoon rolling in the field went unremarked. Or if Ma noticed, she didn't mention them nor chide the children. Annie noticed glances exchanged between her parents, but she couldn't read them. They weren't excited exchanges of information that foretold something interesting, like the night before a special feast day or the days leading up to when Rob and Sarah had been born. No, these looks were conveyed with shiny eyes. As if tears might easily follow.

The next day was Sunday and as usual, the Trents walked together to the ancient stone church in the village. Annie didn't like the priest. He frightened her with his threats of hell and eternal fires if people sinned. She did her best to behave but it was hard. Sometimes she knew she was guilty of the sin of pride. And dishonesty. And wrath. Yes, most of all, wrath.

As much as she loved Rob and Sarah, occasionally, they annoyed her. Ma shared her love equally between the four children, but the younger ones often required more of her attention. So, sometimes, Annie felt the urge to do something to show she was worthy of Ma's time too. That sin was called pride. And sometimes, her efforts were bolstered by a small amount of exaggeration or indeed, lies. When her attempts to gain Ma's notice went unrewarded, she'd occasionally indulged in a temper tantrum.

Once Annie had calmed down, Ma had usually sighed and gently warned her that she must guard against the sin of wrath that her hair colouring might lead her into.

"Like kindling for a fire," she'd often observed with sad eyes as she'd stroked her hair. "You must guard against it, Annie. Douse the flames of your wrath."

Annie wondered what her hair colour had to do with anger, but it was like a lot of things that adults knew. Unquestionable. Baffling. She'd told Ma that it was most unfair that part of her body might attempt to trick her to sin.

But the priest's sermon that Sunday wasn't about pride or wrath or any of the other awful sins. It was about charity. A message that appeared to upset Ma more than ever. And after the service, it seemed that people had been strangely touched by the words and felt the need to place a kindly hand on Ma's shoulder or shake Pa's hand. And Ben and Annie were patted sympathetically on the head.

"Why is everyone so sad?" Sarah asked on the way home to the farm, but she didn't receive a reply.

The next morning, the late summer sun bravely shone in through the windows, but nothing was able to pierce the gloom inside the kitchen. Pa lingered, getting in Ma's way but she didn't scold the way she usually would have. Sarah and Rob squabbled over the puppies, but Ma merely parted the children and put one at either end of the table to eat their meal. They poked out their tongues at each other until they, too, became aware of the atmosphere in the kitchen and stopped misbehaving.

Annie forced down the last of her porridge. She had no appetite but somehow, she knew she must behave well. Something had changed. Was life going to be like this from now on? Ben's eyes darted about as if looking for clues as to why their parents were so on edge. He obviously didn't know either.

"Why are Ben and Annie wearing new clothes?" Sarah asked.

"Curiosity killed the cat." Was Ma's only comment.

The knock on the door made everyone jump.

Ma's hand flew to her chest and her eyes opened wide in alarm. Pa grunted and strode to the door, opening it wide as if he was expecting someone. The man who'd visited several weeks ago bade him good day. It was the same man who'd delivered the clothes that had drawn Sarah's attention.

The stranger entered and taking off his tricorne hat, he bowed politely. Ma curtseyed and Pa bowed too. Annie had never seen her parents so flustered and ill-at-ease. But judging by his fine clothes and bearing, this man was obviously someone of class.

"May I offer you refreshment, Mr Squires, sir?" Ma fidgeted with the edge of her apron.

He politely declined and after withdrawing a pouch of coins from the pocket of his dark blue knee-length coat, he placed it on the table with a jingle.

At the sight of the money, both Ma and Pa started to speak.

"If there's any way we could keep—"

"Would they perhaps allow me to keep the boy as an apprentice—"

Hope shone in their eyes.

The man slowly shook his head. "I took the requests you made on my last visit to the board, but the gentlemen considered it right that the children return to receive an education." He nodded in agreement. "Indeed, it only remains for me to thank you, on behalf of the Foundling Hospital Board, for your splendid care." He looked Annie and Ben up and down and smiled, obviously satisfied. "So, children, shall we take our leave?"

Pa groaned. With a sob, Ma gathered them both into her arms and held them tightly. "You must go with Mr Squires. He will explain everything. I love you. Now, be good children," she whispered.

Mr Squires held out his hands for Annie and Ben. Neither child moved until Ma gently nudged them towards the visitor and pushed their hands towards his.

Against Annie's palm, the man's was smooth. Not like Ma or Pa's rough hands. Not comforting at all. But once he had hold of them, he walked swiftly out of the kitchen and towards his waiting carriage. His coachman took two small bags of belongings from Ma and followed Mr Squires.

Annie turned her head to look back at her parents standing in the doorway. Pa had his arm around Ma's shoulders while she held her apron to her face as if she couldn't bear to look.

Annie caught sight of Ben's face. It had drained of colour and his eyes were huge. They exchanged frightened glances. But Ma had told them to go with the man and at least they were together. Annie couldn't have borne it if they'd been parted. The man had said they were to receive an education. She remembered the priest talking about the school in town although Ma had never mentioned anything about it. Well, it was only a few miles to town. It wouldn't take long and then they'd be able to return home.

CHAPTER 3

Annie didn't remember ever having seen such a grand carriage. It was drawn by four fine horses. Nothing like the sturdy brown horse that belonged to Pa. The top was open, and it could seat four passengers – two facing forwards and two backwards. Mr Squires helped them in, and they sat rigidly behind the coachman's raised bench looking back at the farmhouse. Mr Squires sat in the rear, looking forwards. As they turned out of the narrow, rutted lane from the farmhouse, Annie steadied herself by grasping the seat. Ben did the same and as their little fingers touched, he wrapped his over hers, hooking them together and gripping her tightly. Annie wished she could link arms with Ben and not let go until they were brought home, but it probably wouldn't be wise to draw Mr Squires' attention. He smiled at them from time to time in a kindly way. She thought he had the air of someone important, like the priest. But Annie didn't like the priest. If only Ma was there to explain it all to them.

At the crossroads, they hadn't turned right towards town but carried on. Next to her, Ben began to fidget, and she knew he, too, was wondering where they were going.

The sun had passed its highest point and was beginning to slide down towards the west by the time they arrived at what Mr Squires referred to as their 'new home'. He suggested they sit one on either side of him so they could face forwards and see it as they approached. *New home.* Annie's chest felt as though it was being crushed. She didn't want a new home. Nevertheless, she and Ben unlinked fingers and did as he bade, sitting upright, one on either side of Mr Squires as he pointed out the buildings at the end of the wide road. They hardly needed pointing out. They were enormous.

Straight ahead, were three brick-built structures. One ornate wall in the middle with two gatehouses on either side and between them, large open gates through which Annie caught sight of the grandest buildings she'd ever seen. Two long ones on either side of a huge courtyard and a chapel at the end. Out of the corner of her eye, she saw Ben crane his neck to get a better view and she heard him gasp. More than ever, now, she wished their fingers were still hooked together but when the carriage pulled up, two women wearing what she later learnt were nurses' uniforms met them and one took her hand as she alighted. Ben was being helped out of the other side of the carriage and she lost sight of him.

It would be some time before she saw Ben again.

Faces. Large faces, inches from hers.

Adults bending to her height and peering at her. Well-meaning looks – kind, searching, efficient.

Inspection of her eyes, ears, hair, skin.

"Open wide. Poke out your tongue."

Questions. More questions while a pen scraped across paper, recording everything about her.

Then, the shame of having her hair shaved off. Auburn locks lay scattered on the floor like autumn leaves before they were swept up by a nurse.

"We can't be too careful," Matron said. "Lice and other pests. It'll grow soon enough." She placed the cap back on Annie's head and patted it.

The feel of the fabric against her scalp was strange but Annie was too shocked to cry. She pulled the sides of her cap down to hide the nakedness. But no one seemed to take any notice.

Everywhere was so grand. High ceilings, rich polished wood, fancy fireplaces and walls covered with wonderful, framed paintings.

As they moved from room to room, Annie couldn't believe the number of young girls all dressed the same as her. Some taller, shorter, thinner, fatter.

Her mind blurred with the images. It was all too much to take in. So much noise. So much movement. She tried to make sense of it all and to search the sea of faces for Ben's and when she realised there were no boys amongst them, she asked Matron.

"Your brother? Oh, I see. You mean the boy with whom you arrived? Ah, you won't find him here in the east wing."

"Where is he, please, ma'am?"

"Why, bless you, child. He'll be in the west wing." It was said as if the answer was obvious.

Wings belonged on birds and butterflies. And east and west had once been the places where the sun rose in the morning and sank at night. Now it represented something she couldn't explain that separated her from the only person she'd recognise. The only person in this hospital that she knew. Indeed, the only person in this hospital she loved and longed – beyond all reason – to cling to.

Finally, the tests were finished, and Matron seemed satisfied with the paperwork. The new girl, Anne Sherrington, was pronounced healthy.

A nurse knocked at the door and ushered in a tall, bony girl with brown wisps of hair escaping from her cap.

"Anne Sherrington, I would like you to meet Harriet Feltham, she will take care of you for the next few days. She will show you around. Your bed is next to hers. Perhaps you will even become friends..." Matron smiled at them and with a wave, dismissed them.

Annie allowed Harriet to take her hand and lead her from the room but once outside the door, she burst into tears.

"There, there." Harriet put her arm around Annie's shoulders. "It'll all be better now. You're safe 'ere. They won't beat you. No need to fret."

When Annie didn't stop sobbing, she added, "You get fed an' you get clothed. And one day they'll find you a position in a great house as a maid. So, you see, it's fine."

"But I want to go home to my family," Annie wailed.

"Why?" Harriet sounded surprised. Her brows drew together as she peered at Annie. "I told you, it's nice here. You won't ever get beaten." Harriet looked down at her hands and placed one over the other.

"But I never got beaten at home." Annie looked at the older girl in confusion. "Ma slapped me once or twice, but it was no more than I deserved. No one ever beat me, though."

Harriet took Annie's hand again. Her expression saying that she'd tried her best to comfort the new girl but if she stubbornly resisted any help, that was hardly her fault.

"This is the eating room," she said as she led Annie into a long room full of tables flanked by benches. The smell of cold porridge and boiled cabbage hung in the air.

"So, you never got beaten where you were?" Harriet didn't wait for a reply before adding, "I got beat all the time. I was sent to a woman what took a dislike to me. Hit me with a stick, she did. On me 'ands." She let go of Annie's hand and displayed the backs of hers.

Annie gasped at the scars and faint red stripes that criss-crossed the girl's skin.

"Lucky for me, an inspector saw the marks an' brought me home early. I was only four when I was brought back. An' I overheard Matron tell the inspector that the hospital won't never send babies to that woman again. That were three years ago. I'm seven now." She smiled again as if she'd somehow triumphed.

Before Annie could further examine the scars, Harriet slid her hands beneath her apron.

"This is the way to the kitchen," she announced as if showing a guest around her own house.

Dodging through the steaming, busy kitchen, she took Annie to the yard behind, and showed her the laundry and scullery sheds.

"You'll most likely work in the laundry or kitchen. I work in the laundry."

Annie's head swam. All feeling and thought drained away. Like the washing Ma had done in the old, wooden tub, it felt as though Annie's mind was being pressed down deep into something warm and soapy that was removing every inch of familiar dirt. When her mind came out, she felt it would be clean – and empty. Everything she'd learnt at Ma's was being rubbed away – gently but firmly. A world had been presented to her with so many new ideas that made no sense, she wanted to close her eyes and refuse to take in anything more.

Harriet had been beaten and she now considered this hospital her home. Annie was pleased that Harriet felt safe. The hospital was obviously a good place. But what did it have to do with Annie? Her life had been different. Kind and loving. She belonged with Ma and Pa. She belonged with Rob and Sarah. And so did Ben. At the thought of them all and their welcoming farmhouse, fresh tears slid down her cheeks.

Harriet stopped and with a click of her tongue and an irritated shake of her head, she waited until Annie had stopped crying.

"If you like, I'll show you where we play," she said as if that might cheer Annie up. She led her outside to the colonnade. A young girl was sweeping the area and Annie noticed on the other side of the courtyard a similar building with a colonnade. Harriet followed her gaze.

"Is that the west wing?" Annie asked.

"Yes."

"And is that where the boys play?" Annie pointed at the mirror image of the arcade in which they stood.

Harriet nodded. "We're not allowed to talk to them though."

"But—"

"Who wants to talk to boys anyway?" Harriet snorted in derision.

That night, Annie lay awake in her bed, listening to the sighs and snuffles of the girls in the long dormitory. In the bed next to her, Harriet's breathing was even and deep. Annie longed for the comfort of Sarah's small, plump body pressed against hers. She yearned for the kiss that Ma always placed on her forehead after her prayers. And for the knowledge that on the morrow, she'd wake up at the farm.

Snatches of conversation echoed through her mind. She wanted to believe they were all lies but she was learning that truth became true if everyone believed it to be so. In the hospital, everyone saw things differently from the way she'd believed the world to be. She'd thought

Ma and Pa were her parents. According to Harriet, they'd simply been looking after her until she'd been old enough to return to the Foundling Hospital. Her brother, Ben, wasn't her brother at all. Neither was she related to Rob and Sarah.

"So, who is my mother?" she'd asked Harriet, her head still spinning.

But Harriet had shrugged. "Who knows? You're a foundling. Your ma left you here and then took off."

It couldn't be true. She was in the Foundling Hospital, so it must mean she was a foundling. And yet...

Thoughts chased each other through her head until morning.

When the bell rang at six o'clock, it seemed as if Annie had only been asleep for a few minutes. She was used to rising early but in her other life, there had been time to tickle Sarah or to chase her down the stairs pretending to be a monster. Now, before she'd really woken up, prayers were being read and Annie was on her knees by the side of her bed like every other girl in the dormitory.

Wash, inspection and then they were called to breakfast, after which, the morning was spent in school. Following dinner, it was back to school. But then, to Annie's relief, they were allowed to play outside for an hour until supper at six o'clock. She filed outside and stood by a column, studying the boys in the colonnaded area outside the west wing. It appeared they were following a similar routine to the girls. Finally, she saw Ben standing against the wall, scanning the girls for her. Her frantic wave drew a scowl from the woman who was supervising but Annie had the satisfaction of seeing Ben return her greeting. Knowing he was across the courtyard was such comfort. Annie glared at the back of the woman who'd frowned and wagged a finger at her. Annie bunched her fists and clamped her jaw. No one was going to keep her from Ben. Of course, she'd have to be careful. Clearly, she couldn't stroll across the courtyard to him. But she'd find a way of seeing him. So much had been taken from her but she wouldn't allow them to take Ben.

CHAPTER 4

Gradually, the day's rigid routine became familiar to Ben. He'd been in the hospital for a week and a day. It had been bewildering at first but now he understood the rhythms. The food was sufficient. Plain and dull. But there was enough to satisfy him. The schoolwork was hard, and on several occasions, he'd been smacked across his knuckles. But if the other boys had mastered reading, there was no reason why he shouldn't.

The best part of the day was after school had finished and they were allowed an hour outside to play before supper. He'd earned a slap the first time he'd waved at Annie, having been caught by the schoolmaster. Now, he was more careful. He waited in the same spot by the end column until Annie had assumed the same position and then, he raised his cap as if adjusting it. Annie did the same. That small gesture meant, "Hello. How are you? I'm well. Or as well as can be expected."

It was the best part of his day.

On Sunday, the boys had been taken to the chapel that lay at the far end of the courtyard, separating the east and west wing. Seated with the children in a gallery overlooking the grand people in the pews below, Ben caught sight of Annie. Her head was moving as if she was searching for something and when she spotted him, their eyes had locked. Well, they would have locked had they been closer. He could barely see her. But it had been enough to realise she'd been looking for him.

He wondered how she was coping. She'd had her hair shorn – like him – and he knew she'd have hated that. How long would it be before he could see the beautiful colour of her hair when she moved her cap and not her pale scalp? He ran his hand over his stubble and knew that it would be a few weeks yet.

Would her lack of hair mean a corresponding decrease in her fiery nature? Ma had always blamed Annie's red hair for her quick temper. He immediately replaced the image of Ma's face in his mind with something else. Anything else. If he didn't think about what he'd left behind and didn't consider the future, he wouldn't cry.

After the health checks at his admission, Matron told one of the older boys to look after Ben. Oliver Wills was tall, broad and not afraid of the other boys. He'd been a good choice because he'd taken to Ben and offered his protection. Ben hadn't liked to imagine what life might have been like had Oliver not taken to him.

"It don't do to think about the past. Leave it where it is." Had been Oliver's advice and then he'd added something most astonishing. "A mother what gives her child away ain't worth the worrying about."

Ben had explained that he'd been taken from his mother by Mr Squires. She hadn't given him away at all. And then with a voice dripping with all the experience of his seven years, Oliver had explained.

At first, Ben hadn't believed him. Then he thought back over the years. Men had come to the Trent's house regularly for as long as he could remember, bringing new clothes for him and Annie. There'd been health inspections and questions after which, lots of notes had been taken. Ben had always felt as though he was being watched and judged. It seemed that the men had been there to check that he and Annie were being well cared for and healthy. For the first time, he realised that Rob and Sarah had never been subjected to the questions and probing fingers. When the inspectors had departed, they'd left pouches of coins on the kitchen table for the people Ben had thought were his parents.

And now, he and Annie were here in the Foundling Hospital. Everything pointed to Oliver's explanation being true. And yet...

A new thought. If Oliver was right, then, shortly after Ben had been born, his mother had brought him to this hospital and handed him over. Then she'd walked through the gate and away, leaving him no clue as to his beginnings.

If he'd allowed himself to think about it, he'd have cried with rage. Or perhaps with grief. But he wasn't going to allow himself to think about it.

Oliver had told him that in a few years, he'd be apprenticed. One day, he'd find employment and earn money. He'd be independent. And then, he'd find Annie and they'd live together. He'd look after her and they wouldn't need to worry about where they'd come from and who'd abandoned them. They'd live a comfortable life together. He'd buy a field with an apple tree, and they'd climb it and pick apples then lay on the grass like they'd done with Rob and Sarah just before... No. He wouldn't allow himself to remember the last day they'd played together, or he knew he'd cry.

In the meantime, he'd do whatever was necessary to one day be with Annie. And if that meant learning to read, then he was determined to do so.

During the night he often woke covered in cold sweat. He dreamt of a faceless woman as shadowy as smoke who walked away from him. His mother? He watched her glide away without a backward glance. "Go away," he whispered. She'd rejected him and he wouldn't allow the shadow of her memory to touch him.

During the next few weeks, Ben's reading and writing improved and he received fewer reprimands from the schoolmaster. Life was full. Ruled by the bell with no time for daydreaming or loitering. The most important part of his day was during the hour of recreation when he saw Annie and he sensed it was the same for her too.

So, on the morning he was told he was to spend a few days at an infirmary, he was frantic. Annie wouldn't know where he was. Would she believe he hadn't bothered to look for her?

But there was no choice. All children had to be inoculated against smallpox for the benefit of everyone. An epidemic might result in many deaths. Ben had expressed his fear of being cut and having something that would cause an infection like smallpox rubbed into it, and Oliver had laughed.

"I've had it," he said proudly tapping his arm. "There's only one thing worse than them givin' you one of them inoccerations..." he pulled a serious face. "And that's if you get real smallpox." He ran the tip of his finger across his throat. "Pfft. You're finished."

Ben was certain that wasn't true. He knew of one boy who'd survived the smallpox he'd caught while he was with his wet nurse. But many children who'd caught it had died.

When he'd heard about the boy who'd survived, it wasn't the smallpox that had filled his mind. It was the fact that he'd been living with a wet nurse. The woman Ben had thought of as his mother had been one of those. When the realisation came, he wasn't sure how to feel. Ma had fed him and looked after him as if he'd been her own. He knew that from seeing her with Rob and then Sarah. And yet... He pushed all thoughts away. That was the past. He must believe that sometime in the future he'd make things better. And he could only do that if he didn't allow himself to remember...

The previous week, he'd wondered whether it might be a good idea not to signal to Annie each day during their time of play. She was part of his past and when he saw her, there was always a feeling of longing that drew at his insides. Of course, he didn't want to forget her. She would be his future. When he was a successful man, he'd find her and look after her. But he didn't like the memories that flooded through him when he saw her.

However, the sight of the lonely figure, her neck craning as she looked out for him, had weakened his determination and he'd hurried to the end pillar and raised his hat. She'd lingered then, as if it had upset her so much that when he'd appeared, she'd wanted to hold on to him for longer. It had earned her a reprimand from the supervisor. Annie had walked away but she'd glanced over her shoulder to confirm he was still there and that had persuaded him that despite the pain he felt in remembering his former life when he saw her, he couldn't – wouldn't – stop seeing her.

Except that now, he'd be in the infirmary until the doctors decided he was ready to return to the hospital and Annie wouldn't know where he was.

Ben had fretted so much to get back to the Foundling Hospital, he'd wondered if the doctor would believe he was ill and keep him back. He couldn't bear to think of Annie watching and waiting each evening in vain. He was so relieved to be back that after school, he hurried out to stand by his pillar. Annie wasn't there and his chest tightened at the thought that she might have given up on him appearing again. She might believe he didn't care...

Then, he saw her. She ran to the pillar and took off her cap and waved it back and forth. He did the same.

Annie had been pleased to see him and he felt guilty that he might have caused her worry. Of course, he'd had no choice. He had no choice about anything. As he climbed into bed that night, hot, stinging tears brimmed in his eyes and images filled his mind. Annie with Ma, Pa, Rob and Sarah sitting down for Sunday dinner. He could hear the laughter, smell the roast lamb and almost reach out and touch them. He wiped his eyes angrily on his sleeve. Pictures such as those, he could not allow. He would not allow them. Instead, he imagined it was night-time in the farmhouse kitchen. Darkness had fallen and everyone had gone to bed. The table was empty. The room was cold. And that was how it must remain in his memory. He wouldn't think of the past – he must only think of the future.

But that was too difficult to imagine. He had no idea how Annie would look when she grew up. Instead, he brought to mind the image of her on that Sunday when she'd peered down through the branches of the apple tree, with leaves caught in her copper-gold hair and her eyes alight with excitement. Yes, she would be his future. But even though he'd made a decision, everything was still so uncertain. The only things he could control were his actions and he would do his best. Ma had always told him to do that.

He pushed Ma's memory away. He would do his best because *he* wanted to.

"That girl..." Oliver said looking at Annie on the other side of the courtyard. Ben had just raised his cap to her, and she'd done the same. Ben's stomach sank. He hadn't wanted anyone to notice his silent conversation with Annie. He'd thought he'd been careful. A lie flew to Ben's lips, but he stopped before it was uttered. It would only draw Oliver's interest further. Ben knew the older boy well enough to know that.

"My sister," said Ben.

"Sister? You mean the girl what was with you when you were staying with your wet nurse? I don't expect she's your sister. Just another foundling."

If Oliver had punched him, Ben couldn't have been more surprised.

Annie had been his first memory. She was part of him. He knew he'd been abandoned, and that Ma and Pa weren't his parents, but he'd always thought of Annie as his sister. Now, the realisation was like a trickle of icy water down his back. Of course. She'd have been the baby who'd been accepted before him. He'd seen the metal tokens that had been fastened around their necks although not understood their significance. And he knew their numbers followed each other. How had he not worked that out before? How could he have been so foolish?

He wanted to punch Oliver for... For what? For telling him the truth? For robbing him of a lie he'd believed to be true? Ben wanted to bury his head in his hands and shut the world out. When he looked up Annie had gone. She'd slipped into the crowd and Ben had to stop himself from running across the courtyard, finding her and holding her tightly. Surely nothing else could be taken from him?

But it had turned out to be a good thing that Oliver had discovered about Annie. A few weeks before, Oliver had followed one of the older boys after lights out and they'd crept behind the chapel and made their way to the east side. Around the kitchen courtyard were the scullery, storage sheds and laundry, in which there was a small window. The older boy had been sweet on a laundry maid and he'd spoken to her through the small window.

Shortly after, the boy had been apprenticed to a bookbinder and had left the hospital. But Oliver knew it was possible to speak to girls.

Would Ben like to speak to Annie?

Oh, yes!

Then, Oliver would try to help.

He'd kept his word and had arranged for one of the laundry maids to carry a message to Annie to meet Ben at midnight on Sunday. Ben had slipped out of the dormitory at ten to twelve, his heart beating furiously not only at the thought of possibly seeing Annie but because he wasn't sure whether Oliver was trying to get him into trouble.

Admittedly, Oliver had been trustworthy so far but in this strange shifting world where things were always something other than what you expected them to be, who could tell?

And anyway, what was the chance that Annie would also be able to slip away from her dormitory unnoticed? He wondered if she'd be too afraid, and then he'd smiled. His Annie had been afraid of nothing. And then he'd stopped abruptly. His Annie hadn't been afraid of anything *then*. This was now. Annie might be very different.

To his amazement, he made it out of the west wing without being caught. His ears strained to pick up any sound that would tell him he'd been betrayed. In the distance he could hear the revelry from Tottenham Court with its many lively inns. Much closer, were voices from the skittle ground of a nearby alehouse. A dog barked, and feet away, something with tiny claws scuttled over stones. Possibly a rat. Ahead, two tiny points of light glistened in the darkness. A soft miaow told him it was one of the hospital cats, probably after that rat.

Ben crept onward through the night grateful to the full moon for casting some light into the shadows behind the chapel. When he arrived at the tiny window, he wanted to cry. It was high up in the wall and there was no way he could look through. A sound sent him scrambling for the shadows until he saw the window open. A rush of elation coursed through him as he saw Annie's beautiful face appear.

"Ohhh!" she sighed, and that single sound told him how much she'd longed to be with him. He held his hands up to her as if she could jump into them. Foolish, because the window was too small for her to climb through. However, she stretched one hand out and reached down to him. By standing on tiptoe, he could just touch her fingertips. He dared not tarry long. With great excitement, they arranged to meet again the following week.

Miraculously, luck seemed to be with them and each Sunday they managed to meet for a minute or two. It wasn't long enough but it was better than nothing and gradually as time passed, Annie's hair grew back to the thick auburn locks he remembered, and he didn't need to stand on tiptoe to reach her hand and to grasp it tightly.

CHAPTER 5

1781

It had been two weeks since Annie had seen Ben. He'd left the Foundling Hospital, having been apprenticed to a boatbuilder.

Good riddance. She never wanted to see him again.

She couldn't believe what she'd heard him say about her. It had been hateful.

She'd arrived at the laundry and had moved the box beneath the window, then climbing up, she'd opened it slightly. It was early. She'd been impatient to spend some time with Ben, not having seen much of him during the church service earlier. Since his friend, Oliver, had been apprenticed to a blacksmith, she'd worried about Ben, knowing that he was sometimes picked on by the other boys. She'd heard them taunt him, calling him 'Ape' and 'Monkey'. So cruel. It was true that he had thick dark hair and that his skin was swarthy but in her eyes, he was handsome. He was perfect – not someone who should be likened to an animal.

Josiah Grant, an older boy was now often to be seen with Ben. Josiah had been apprenticed to a joiner for two years but had returned to the hospital when his master had died and the widow had turned him out. Now, the other boys seemed to leave Ben alone but still, Annie was worried. There was something about the way that Ben stood – with shoulders hunched and head lowered as if he was dreading someone hitting him. She'd asked him about it the previous Sunday through the window, but he'd instantly looked away when she'd remarked that he didn't seem happy. Perhaps he was worried that if Josiah was sent away, the others would start mocking him again. Well, thank goodness for handsome Josiah with his blond hair and winning smile. Hopefully, he'd keep her Ben safe.

That dreadful Sunday, she'd sat down on the box, waiting for Ben and hoping his week had been better than the last. Alert for any sounds that might result in her being caught, and of course, noises that would tell her Ben was approaching, she'd picked up what sounded like two voices. Quickly, she'd jumped off the box and crept beneath the bench, hiding from anyone who might enter the laundry. But the voices were coming from outside. Sharp, angry hisses.

Annie wondered if Ben had been followed by one of the boys who tormented him. Her chest had grown tighter. If one of them gave Ben away out of spite they'd both be in trouble. There'd be punishment and worse than that, they'd never be allowed to meet again.

"Oh, please..." she'd muttered a silent prayer that they wouldn't be discovered and that there was another explanation for the two angry voices. Crawling out from beneath the bench, she'd climbed back on the box and peeped out of the window. In the moonlight, she'd seen the fair head of Josiah Grant and the shadow that she thought was Ben.

Through the slightly open window, she'd heard Ben say in a shaky voice, "She won't want to know you."

"We'll see. She might not like you, Ape. But she'll undoubtedly want a real man."

Annie had heard the contempt in Josiah's voice.

"Well, I've had her and she's not worth it." Ben's voice had been harsh. Hateful.

Annie's hands had flown to her flaming cheeks. Surely, she'd misheard that. Or misunderstood. Surely Ben hadn't just said what she thought he'd said.

"You?" Josiah's voice had been less certain. "You've had her?"

"Yes. And she's a liar. She's not worth anything. There are lots of other girls much nicer than her. And prettier." Ben's voice had become offhandedly boastful like he was trying to sound grown up.

No, they couldn't be talking about her. Then who?

"But I bet she's fiery, with all that red hair," Josiah had remarked with a course laugh.

"No," said Ben airily. "I've told you. Her hair's ugly. She's nothing much. If I were you, I wouldn't bother."

"Then why do you come each Sunday?"

"I don't."

"Where d'you go then?"

"Oh. Here and there." The tone had been casual. Vague. But it suggested something exciting.

"If it's so wonderful, take me there."

"Very well. Next week."

"So, why did you come here tonight, Ape?"

There was silence for a few moments, then Ben lowered his voice further and whispered, "Look! Up there, a light. Best we go back to the dormitory."

"Where? I can't see it." But Josiah had sounded nervous.

Annie had heard the two boys creep away. She'd climbed on the box and poked her head out of the window, unwilling and unable to believe it had been Ben. But as two figures had slipped into the shadows, the dark one had looked over his shoulder. It had definitely been Ben.

Annie had crept back to bed, rage pushing away all reason, and had cried herself to sleep. She never wanted to see Ben again. And from his own lips, she'd heard that he'd be taking Josiah somewhere much more interesting. Perhaps to an alehouse in nearby Tottenham Court. Is that where he'd gone when he'd left her each Sunday? How had she never seen this side of Ben before? Well, she'd never see it again, that was certain.

It wouldn't have been of any account if Annie had wanted to see Ben again because two days later, he was sent away from the Foundling Hospital. His apprenticeship had begun with Charles Wilson, of C. Wilson & Co, Shipwrights in Rotherhithe, south of the River Thames.

Ben had intended to tell Annie about all about it on that final Sunday evening and to give her the present he'd made. There hadn't been much time to prepare as he'd only discovered about the apprenticeship two days before, but he'd found a piece of wood in the carpenter's workroom and fashioned it into a disc. It wasn't completely round but it had been the best he could do at such short notice. On one face, he'd scratched a heart and inside it, he'd inscribed her Foundling Hospital identification number, 16,700. The other side was identical, but the number was 16,701 – his number. He'd also picked her a flower in the hospital vegetable garden where he'd been working on Saturday.

It had been such bad luck that Josiah had heard him get out of bed that night. Ben had probably been so eager to see Annie and give her his gifts that he hadn't taken as much care as usual. Occupying the last bed in the dormitory – the one closest to the door had been perfect. No one wanted the position because of the chilly drafts that blew in during the winter, so Ben hadn't been challenged for the bed. But on that night, of all nights, Josiah had spotted him and followed at a distance. By the time Ben had realised the older boy was trailing him, he was behind the chapel. There was nowhere else to go and knowing the laundry was nearby and that there was a window, Josiah had come to the correct conclusion. Or perhaps Ben hadn't been as clever as he thought he'd been and others knew where he went and who he met.

Ben hadn't wanted to anger Josiah whose fists were large and powerful. Life was becoming difficult with the bully often picking on him. The other boys joined in now that Oliver had gone, and Ben was often covered in cuts and bruises caused by Josiah. So, he didn't want to tell him to go away.

Neither did he want to go back to bed – that evening would be his only opportunity to tell Annie about his apprenticeship. He also wanted to assure her he'd be back for her when he'd gained employment and could look after her. He'd never revealed his plans to her before but when he told her, he knew she'd be pleased. If he couldn't speak to her that night, he risked being sent away without her knowing what had happened to him. And that would be unthinkable.

So, it had seemed worth the risk to anger Josiah. After all, if he was leaving on Tuesday he'd finally be out of the bully's way. He could do his worst to Ben on Monday but after that, Ben would be gone. So, nervously, he told Josiah to go away. He was tempted to hit him but if there was a fight, they'd both be discovered, and Ben would be no closer to telling Annie his news.

And then he had an idea. He'd feign indifference. If he pretended not to care, then perhaps Josiah would lose interest. But the older boy wasn't fooled. Somehow, he'd known Ben was going to see Annie. And worse still, he told Ben he was going to take a personal interest in her.

The blood almost froze in Ben's veins when he'd seen the lewd wink. He'd inadvertently led Josiah to Annie and now she'd be in danger. And Ben wouldn't be there to protect her. The blood that had seemed to stop now pounded in his ears.

Think, think!

But there was no time. Words flew to his lips. If he could persuade Josiah that Annie was worthless, then perhaps he'd leave her alone.

"She won't want to know you," he'd said. Well, that clearly wasn't going to work with someone like Josiah. That was a challenge and the handsome boy had been with several of the kitchen maids, Ben knew. And then, before he'd realised what he was saying, he'd pretended... he couldn't even form the words inside his head. It was unspeakable. And yet, it seemed that he'd persuaded Josiah that Annie really wasn't worth any effort.

And then, in desperation, he'd pretended he'd seen a light in the west wing and that had been enough to persuade Josiah to follow him away from Annie. But that last look over his shoulder had shown him her face at the laundry window. When he'd seen her horrified expression, he realised she must have heard – if not every word of the conversation – then enough for her to know the dreadful claims that he'd made. As if he was boasting. And insulting her. Being hateful.

Now, he wouldn't have an opportunity to explain how – far from intending to shame her – he'd been trying to protect her. Nor would he be able to tell her about his apprenticeship and his dreams for when it was over. The flower and wooden token he'd wanted to give her had been dropped in the scuffle with Josiah and were now lost somewhere behind the chapel where the cats roamed.

It had been from Verity, one of the laundry maids, that Annie learnt that a master joiner had been found who'd agreed to take Josiah Grant as his apprentice.

"He said he'd marry me!" Verity wailed when she found out he'd gone.

"Told me the same," said Hannah, another laundry maid, with a toss of her head. "Reckon he told a few more too. Good riddance I say."

But Verity wouldn't be consoled.

Blond-haired, handsome Josiah had broken a few hearts.

"Are you sure he's going to a joiner?" Hannah asked, "I heard he were going to a shipwrights'. It'd be just like him to deceive everyone."

"He's definitely going to be a joiner. It's that boy what the others call 'Ape' what went to a shipwrights'. Down near Rotherhithe, I hear. But Josiah's gone to Wapping," Verity said as she wiped her eyes.

Annie thrust the sheets into the soapy water, forcing them beneath the surface and squeezed the fabric in her fists.

"You tryin' to strangle them sheets?" Hannah asked.

"No." Annie released her grip and relaxed her clenched jaw.

So, Ben had gone.

He hadn't said goodbye although to be fair, he'd probably come on Sunday evening to do that. So, why had he said all those awful things about her?

Ben and Josiah. Untrustworthy. Well, she wouldn't let it affect her. She would... She stopped, realising with surprise that she didn't know what she'd do. Since she'd arrived in the hospital, life had been organised for her. Bells had rung out, governing her day. There were rules. She could talk while working in the laundry but not at meals. She must not leave the hospital grounds. There was no need to think, her life was laid out for her. The only independent thought she'd had was for Ben. And now, she didn't ever want to see his stupid face again. Ape.

A tear slid down her nose and dripped into the water as she bent over the tub, rubbing the sheets vigorously. She needed to think about herself. What would happen to her? Not that she had any say in the matter but at least she could be prepared. In a year or two, she'd be apprenticed. Not to any of the places open to the boys like rope-making, gardening or book binding, but to a housekeeper in a rich man's house.

But now, she felt like a rudderless boat. She hadn't given the future much thought before. Where she'd be in five years' time. Ten years. Who she'd be with. But now that Ben had gone from her life and her heart, she realised that without knowing it, she'd always assumed he'd be part of her future. But no longer. Time stretched ahead of her like the sea at night. Dark, deep and reaching into the unknown.

Until someone told her what was to become of her, she must be patient. She lifted the sheet out of the tub and squeezed out the excess water. How many more sheets would she wash until that time came?

It turned out to be not many sheets at all.

CHAPTER 6

Mrs Barrett, the housekeeper, gripped the banister and groaned as she reached the top of the enormous, sweeping staircase. She paused, allowing the pain in her knees to subside. Years ago, when she'd first arrived at the Duke of Westervale's mansion in Mayfair as a nursery maid, she'd been as slim as a reed. But the Duke looked after his servants well and nowadays, she was considerably larger and required a sturdy maid to lace up her garments. With all that extra bulk, it was becoming harder to heft all her weight up such a long flight of stairs. But needs must. The guest bedrooms in the east wing had to be examined. Standards must be maintained. The Duke would expect it even though his health was failing. As was hers.

They were neither getting any younger. Her mind was filled with foreboding. Her eldest sister had died the previous month. How much longer did she have left? It was possible she'd have years, but who other than the Almighty could tell?

She walked along the corridor, observing tables, priceless vases and oil paintings in ornate frames with a practised eye. She would not tolerate dust and made a mental note to chastise the maid who should have dusted this hall and all its expensive contents. Hopefully, His Grace's brother's bedroom would be cleaner. Lord Henry and his wife, Lady Constance, would be arriving on Saturday.

Bloodsuckers, the pair of them.

They'd evidently heard that His Grace was indisposed and had come to see how close to death he was. Not close enough for their liking, Mrs Barrett would wager. The Duke and his younger brother did not agree on anything. And as for that dreadful woman Constance Farringdon... Mrs Barrett sniffed. Such a hard woman. Like flint.

Well, she would not give them cause for complaint. Everything in Tavistock Hall would be perfect, she'd see to that.

But if anything should happen to His Grace... She clenched her jaw and scowled at the thought of his feckless younger brother, Lord Henry, becoming the Duke of Westervale and his wife becoming the Duchess.

Mrs Barrett snorted. If that happened, she'd immediately hand in her notice. She'd already made plans to live in Essex with her widowed sister, Patience.

Tragically, His Grace did not have a living heir. Various children had died in infancy although one son and one daughter had survived to adulthood. The son had died of consumption many years before and then there'd been Lady Margaret...

Mrs Barrett's groan of despair echoed along the hall. Sometimes it felt as though a great weight was pressing down on her. Perhaps that was why her knees hurt so badly. For years, they'd borne the weight of the guilty secret she'd never divulged. Not that the realisation of what was causing the pain helped. It wasn't a secret she had any business sharing and anyway, telling anyone wouldn't have halved the burden. She had no choice but to keep faith with Lady Margaret.

Although... A new thought drifted into her mind as insubstantial as mist. She placed her hand on the doorknob of Lord Henry and Lady Constance's room and paused while the idea took shape. If His Grace had an heir, it was unlikely his brother and unpleasant wife would be visiting. She alone knew the Duke did have an heir. Well, possibly not an heir. Mrs Barrett was unclear whether His Grace's granddaughter would inherit anything, and she'd thought it unwise to ask in case she inadvertently gave anything away. But there was a child of his line. A quick calculation told her the child would now be almost thirteen. If she was still alive, of course. So many children died in infancy. The Foundling Hospital had a good reputation for cleanliness and health care. Otherwise, Lady Margaret would not have allowed her child to go there. But even so...

A longing deep inside Mrs Barrett welled up. How she missed Lady Margaret. Tears still sprang to her eyes at the thought of the young woman she'd nursed as a baby. Lady Margaret had almost been like her own child. And now a few miles away in a hospital, the daughter of her beloved mistress might well be growing up. The child was like a piece of one of those new-fangled jigsaw puzzles. The only person who knew where all the pieces were and could fit them together to make a picture, was Mrs Barrett. Was it time to act? Might she be too late?

Well, there was only one way to find out.

She quickly checked the rooms to satisfy herself it was aired and clean and then hurried downstairs. There would be time to go out later that afternoon but first, she had things to prepare. Buried deep in a chest in her room was the paper that the secretary had handed to her when she'd left baby Caroline at the hospital. Pinned to it was the scrap of cloth from the baby's gown. Lady Margaret had given Mrs Barrett money before she'd died, not knowing whether at some stage in the future the child could be retrieved and whether there'd be a price for the care the child had received.

Mrs Barrett dropped the money into her bag with the girl's details, one emerald earring and the fabric square. She hid the bag beneath her pillow away from prying eyes and would fetch it once she'd finished her work.

Strangely, the ache in her knees stopped being so troublesome and she noticed a slight spring in her step. That was surely a sign that what she was doing was right. But suppose she angered the Duke? Any man would be shocked to suddenly discover he had a thirteen-year-old granddaughter. Perhaps, rather than bringing the child home and announcing her presence, she should be more circumspect? After all, such a shock might be too much for his delicate heart. No, she'd use her common sense. That was what she did best, and it had taken her from being a nursemaid to becoming a housekeeper. She'd use common sense now. She would bring the child back and hide her for a while. No, that was foolish there were too many members of staff in this house to keep a secret like that.

Yes, she had it! She knew exactly what she was going to do.

Later, she took her bag from its hiding place and strode out of the house in the manner of a woman who did not intend to reveal her destination nor to explain the purpose of her journey.

In the Foundling Hospital, Mrs Barrett stressed the Duke of Westervale's name and reminded Matron that he'd donated a significant amount of money to the institution the previous year. That was sufficient to gain her a brief interview with Mr Fleet, one of the governors.

"I see," Mr Fleet said slowly after he'd matched the letter G on Mrs Barrett's billet with what had been written in the records for that date. "The girl was brought in on the day you stated, the letter, the earring token and the fabric samples match those that we have. But I'm sure you'll appreciate that I will have to take your request to the board of governors. It is somewhat irregular but under the circumstances..."

"And Caroline? Will she be consulted?"

Mr Fleet cleared his throat. "She is no longer called Caroline, Mrs Barrett. She is now Anne Sherrington. It is our policy that all children are given new names on entry to the hospital."

"Quite." Mrs Barrett wondered what Lady Margaret would have made of that. "Will Anne be asked or simply told?"

"We will ask her if she is agreeable to the proposition, but we will not force her. My guess is that she will consent. She is a sensible girl although over the years, from time to time, she has shown a wilful temper. Of late, she has been more subdued, thankfully."

"And she will not be told... everything?"

"If the board agrees to release the girl, I will tell her all she needs to know. Although you are claiming her on behalf of her late mother and her family, she will not be told that. She will simply believe she is your apprentice." A slight frown creased Mr Fleet's brow.

"It's for the best," Mrs Barrett said. "And I trust there will be complete discretion?"

"Of course. The details will be treated with the utmost confidentiality. The Duke has been a most valued benefactor. No one would risk displeasing His Grace."

"Indeed." Mrs Barrett rearranged her gloves in her lap, not wanting to meet Mr Fleet's gaze and possibly give away her anxiety. What would His Grace say if he knew what she was doing? He would not be pleased that she'd given the impression Mrs Barrett was following his orders.

Mr Fleet clasped his hands together as if their business was concluded. "I will write to His Grace and inform him of the governors' decision—"

Mrs Barrett held her hand up. "Sadly, His Grace is currently indisposed and has asked that I deal with this issue. He was most firm on the matter. I would appreciate it if you would write to me..." She held her breath, hoping he wouldn't argue.

"Certainly. I shall ensure a letter is delivered to you with their decision."

Mrs Barrett slowly let out her breath.

As she walked out of the hospital gate, her step seemed even lighter than it had when she'd entered.

CHAPTER 7

Annie couldn't believe it. She was to be apprenticed to the housekeeper of a duke. A new start. Such wondrous luck.

How different would it be from what she was used to? Would she cope? Her first thought was that she must tell Ben. Then the memory of his hurtful words and the realisation that her future would not include him made her stomach sink. Their lives were going in different directions and even if she wanted to see him again – which she decidedly did not – she didn't know where in Rotherhithe he was staying. And, in turn, he wouldn't know she'd be living in a mansion further west, in Mayfair. No, they'd never meet again. Good. Stupid Ape.

Mayfair. She whispered the word, rolling it around in her mouth as if it was a tasty morsel. Mayfair, where the rich lived. Where a duke lived. And where she would soon be living.

When she knew that the housekeeper was coming to take her to her new home, she'd wondered if the carriage would be much grander than the one in which Mr Squires had brought her and Ben to London. It was disappointing to discover it was a Hackney coach. Well, of course. The Duke was hardly likely to have sent a liveried coach and footmen for her.

Mrs Barrett seemed very pleasant. Her round face was framed by grey curls, on top of which was a starched white cap. Unlike Matron, her brown eyes were soft and prone to filling with tears which she constantly dabbed away.

Annie sat with eyes down and her hands in her lap during the journey. Mrs Barratt had asked her how she'd liked the hospital and she'd replied that she'd liked it well enough. Perhaps she should have shown more gratitude because the housekeeper's eyes filled with tears again. Had she said the wrong thing?

Thankfully, Mrs Barratt remained quiet for the rest of the journey and Annie didn't have to worry about answering questions.

Annie looked at the grand houses in the street where the carriage shuddered to a halt. There was a large garden in the middle of the square around which stood stylish buildings, but to her surprise, Mrs Barrett didn't enter any of those houses. She told Annie to follow as she went around the corner. This was a much larger square where the houses were even bigger and more elegant. Then, strangely, with her head down as if she didn't want to be noticed, Mrs Barrett led her to the servants' entrance at the back of the largest mansion of all – Tavistock Hall.

Annie couldn't imagine why Mrs Barrett hadn't simply asked the coachman to draw up outside the mansion. But what did she know about how aristocratic houses were run?

"It ain't fair! You never get a good telling-off. Barrett always catches me doin' something wrong and makes my life a misery. But never you!" Meg, the girl with whom Annie was sharing a room in the attic of Tavistock Hall, angrily brushed her hair.

Annie said nothing. There was no point denying it. She, too, had noticed that Mrs Barrett treated her differently from the other maids. It had made her very unpopular amongst the other girls.

"Don't know why she likes you so much. You've only been here a year; I've been here three and she don't treat me so well." Meg slammed her brush down on her bedside table.

"Mind you, I don't think her mind's as sharp as it was when I first started." Meg wiggled her finger near her temple. "Now, sometimes, she don't seem to know what day it is. Although she always sees when I ain't got around to cleaning something."

Annie hadn't been working in Tavistock Hall long enough to be able to judge. Certainly, since she'd arrived, Mrs Barrett had occasionally seemed preoccupied and from time to time, she'd forgotten Annie's name, beginning to call her Catherine or Caroline or some such name. Each time she'd stopped herself and her cheeks had flooded with colour then briskly she'd corrected herself. Immediately, she'd criticised something Annie had done or not done. Annie hadn't taken a great deal of notice. After all, Mrs Barrett had many people under her, and it wasn't surprising if she sometimes muddled people's names. It wasn't until she'd been there many months that she realised there was nobody in Tavistock Hall called Catherine or Caroline. She'd assumed she reminded the housekeeper of someone who looked like her. But in truth, what did it matter?

"I do my best, scrubbing my fingers to the bone, but it's never good enough." Meg got into bed and pulling the blanket up to her chin, she blew out the candle.

Annie climbed into her bed. Mrs Barrett was indeed a puzzle. The malady that had affected Mrs Barrett's eyes when she'd fetched Annie from the hospital had healed although periodically, if Annie turned abruptly, she noticed the housekeeper dabbing her face with a handkerchief. More often than not, Mrs Barrett would turn and walk briskly away, her back straight but the lace of her handkerchief visible in her fist. However, it didn't happen often and overall, life was satisfactory. Although the hours were long and the work was backbreaking, Annie was well fed, and she was allowed time off to do as she pleased.

During their free time, many of the maids went out together and strolled around the Serpentine in Hyde Park. Annie had never been invited to join them. Anyone who hadn't noticed the housekeeper's favouritism was soon enlightened by Meg, and now, the maids displayed their resentment towards Annie by ignoring her and shunning her company. While they were out, Annie read the books Mrs Barrett allowed her to borrow from the library, improving her reading and escaping from real life into wondrous worlds.

One day, Mrs Barrett bustled into the library while Annie was selecting a book. She almost dropped it in alarm. She had permission to be there and to take books but still, she felt guilty as if she had no right to touch anything in the magnificent room, much less to borrow a book and read it.

"You are needed in His Grace's apartment," Mrs Barrett said. She clapped her hands together when Annie simply stared at her. "Come! Now!"

Annie replaced the book with shaking hands and hurried after the housekeeper wondering what she'd be required to do. As a scullery maid, she'd never been expected to clean His Grace's bedroom nor any of the rooms that led off it, so it couldn't be that she'd failed to do something. The most likely explanation was that one of the chamber maids, who was now promenading in Hyde Park, had neglected to do something and Annie was the first maid the housekeeper had come across who might deal with the problem.

Annie followed Mrs Barrett into the Duke's apartment. His Grace was in a small chamber leading off the bedroom, sitting in a chair next to the fire. He had a blanket over his knees despite the room being hot and airless. Mrs Barrett shepherded Annie to the middle of the sumptuous rug where she stood with her toes curling up in her boots as the Duke put on his glasses and scrutinised her. He could only have been staring at her for several seconds, but it seemed to last much longer, and she could almost feel his gaze alight on her face and glide back and forth across her features. She looked down, aware that her cheeks had flushed and that with her red hair and the reflection from the fire, she must have looked as though she were aflame.

Eventually, he cleared his throat and Annie looked up, daring to glance at his face. It was the first time she'd ever seen him close up. Although he was relaxing on his own, he still looked impeccably smart wearing a loose banyan of embroidered silk. Protruding from the blanket were matching silk slippers. But it was his face that held Annie's attention. If she'd thought about him at all, she'd have imagined hard, gimlet eyes set in a haughty, uncaring face. So, she was surprised to see such a gentle expression on his aristocratic features. He seemed to sag slightly, his shoulders drooping and his eyes softening and filling with tears.

He looked at Mrs Barrett and after heaving an enormous sigh, he nodded. A silent communication had passed between them, and Annie held her breath, painfully aware that she had no idea what to do nor how to behave. If she was required to tend a fire or clean a window, she wished that someone would simply tell her.

Annie swung round as the doorknob turned and saw Mrs Barrett leave. Panic bubbled up in her chest. Should she follow? His Grace hadn't dismissed her. She turned back to him, expecting to see irritation and to hear a reprimand but still, he surveyed her silently, his eyes sad, like a puppy dog's.

When he spoke, she jumped even though his voice was gentle. "Can you read, child?"

Annie gulped and nodded. "Y...yes, Your Grace."

"Then sit." He indicated a stool next to his chair.

She hesitated for a second, then, when he smiled, she sat down, sitting stiffly upright.

The Duke passed her a large, open, leather-bound Bible and she placed it on her lap.

"Start here." With one long, slender finger, he pointed to a passage.

The light was dim in the chamber and the text was small.

Annie's mouth had gone dry. "B...but if any provide not for his own, and especially for those of his own house, he hath denied the faith, and is worse than an infidel..."

Annie read haltingly and cringed inside at her voice filling the tiny room. Other than the crackling fire and an occasional sigh from the Duke, it was the only sound.

When she reached the end of the chapter, she looked up to see whether she should continue.

Please let me go now.

The Duke smiled at her. "That will be all, child. You may leave. I fear I'm most weary."

Annie stood abruptly and bobbed a curtsey, hoping he didn't change his mind. When she reached the door, she turned, wondering if she ought to curtsey again but his eyes had closed. A single tear slipped down his cheek, glistening in the firelight.

What was it about this house that caused the people who should be the happiest to be so sad?

After that, Mrs Barrett regularly took Annie to His Grace's chamber to read passages of the Bible to him when the other maids had gone out. Gradually, her voice became less shaky, and she read more confidently. In turn, he lost the dark shadows beneath his eyes and the lines around his mouth softened. Still, no explanation was given as to why a scullery maid had been selected to read to His Grace. And yet, she understood that as much as she wanted to keep the pleasant afternoons spent in his company to herself, the Duke didn't want them discussed in the servants' quarters either. Mrs Barrett ensured she slipped into and out of the room unobserved.

Annie still slept in a room with Meg, but she no longer grumbled about Annie finding favour with Mrs Barrett. She'd met an apprentice in Hyde Park and her head was full of her young man and their plans to marry, leaving no room for resentment of the quiet and unobtrusive girl with whom she shared a bedroom.

One night in the late autumn, as the two maids prepared for bed, Meg groaned. "Next week, we start to prepare for the His Grace's brother's yearly visit." She groaned again. "I swear his wife is a witch."

Annie remembered the previous year having been confined to the kitchen, scouring pots for the duration of their stay. There had been so much food eaten during those six weeks that Cook had been stretched to the limit. She'd almost passed out on several occasions from heat exhaustion and had threatened to hand in her notice twice. Food had to be cooked according to Lord Henry and Lady Constance's taste, and dishes had frequently been sent back to the kitchen for one reason or another. There seemed to be no pleasing the guests.

Lady Constance was the daughter of a Marquess and seemed to assume that now she'd married into a duke's family, she was even more important. Her sense of entitlement resulted in impossibly demanding standards. Her complaints were endless. Mrs Barrett usually got on well with the steward but under the difficult conditions, they had argued, and the dreadful atmosphere had spread throughout the entire house.

What a relief it had been when Lord Henry and his wife had gone. The following day, everyone had relaxed and even Mrs Barrett had lowered her strict standards.

"I swear that woman was drawing up a list of all the paintings in the withdrawing room when she was last here." Meg blew out the candle plunging their tiny bedroom into darkness.

"Why?" Annie asked.

"So that nothing goes missing when she inherits the lot, of course. And I've heard from one of the footmen that the way she looks at His Grace is a scandal. She can barely keep the hope from her eyes."

"Hope?"

"Yes, she and her husband can't wait for the Duke to die."

Annie gasped. It was shocking to hear such words.

Meg ignored her. "Mind you, I swear that this time, she might be in luck."

"Why?"

Meg snorted in disbelief at Annie's naivety.

"Because, by all accounts, His Grace ain't long for this world."

"That's not true!" Annie sat up in bed in the darkness.

"How would you know?" There was a suspicious edge to Meg's voice. Annie's hand flew to her mouth. She knew Meg was a gossip and would home in on any titbits of interesting news.

"I just don't think it's true. That's all." She kept her tone as vague as she could hoping Meg wouldn't ask any questions. But the other girl was too tired to pursue it. After all, what would a lowly scullery maid know?

Annie pulled the blanket up to her chin and lay rigidly until she heard Meg's deep, even breathing. Hopefully, by tomorrow Meg would have forgotten Annie's comment. His Grace did, indeed, appear to be unwell although from time to time his eyes sparkled, and during the last few days, she had the impression that he wasn't so much sick, as weary of life. Just recently he'd given her a prayerbook with a golden clasp that she'd carefully hidden beneath her mattress. That day, he'd instructed her to read the parable about the shepherd who left his flock to search for one lost sheep, and it had seemed to please him greatly. He'd told her she'd read it very well. Strange that it had made him so happy.

The following week, Lord Henry and Lady Constance arrived in their grand carriage with various servants of their own. Annie was disappointed that Mrs Barrett once again sent her to the kitchen. It was going to be one of the busiest and most fraught places in Tavistock Hall for the duration of their guests' stay.

The frenzy of preparations gave way to feverish agitation as the Duke's brother and his wife stepped into the magnificent entrance hall. Over the next few weeks, squabbles broke out between footmen, between maids and between anyone else employed by the Duke to keep the mansion and grounds clean and tidy. Cook scolded everyone who entered the kitchen, including Mrs Barrett and the steward and everyone who could possibly keep out of her way, did so. Even the cats remained in the garden.

Annie worked diligently, scrubbing floors, boiling water and scouring pots and pans with sand. As soon as one meal was over, preparations were underway for the next and Annie was grateful that she was unlikely to lay eyes on the dreaded Lord Henry and his wife. If Meg was correct and they were waiting for His Grace to die so that Lord Henry could claim the title and all the properties and lands, she didn't want to be anywhere near them. The Duke was so gentle and kind. She couldn't bear to think of him gone.

Eight weeks later, when Cook was on the verge of handing in her notice, finally Lord Henry and Lady Constance departed for their home in Yorkshire. They were as ill-tempered as when they'd arrived but everyone in Tavistock Hall rejoiced even if the tips they gave the staff as they left, were miserly.

Petty quarrels were smoothed over and there was a look of relief on every face. Praise God, the Duke was still alive, and the house could relax. However, everyone knew that if His Grace survived for another year, the unpleasant couple would be back.

CHAPTER 8

Over the next few years, Annie was promoted to housemaid and when she was nineteen – to chambermaid. The favour shown to her by Mrs Barrett did nothing for Annie's popularity. And there were also whispers about what went on in the Duke's apartment – the secret of Annie being invited to regularly visit His Grace had finally got out.

Contrary to his brother's hopes, His Grace's health had improved rather than deteriorated and although he wasn't strong, he regained an interest in life. He still didn't venture out of Tavistock Hall but from time to time he attended church.

Annie was aware that she was the topic of much gossip but since no one dared voice their criticisms of her within Mrs Barrett's hearing – and definitely not within His Grace's – she didn't care. Life was good. She loved reading to the Duke when he summoned her to his chamber. He'd taught her to play chess and occasionally he told her about his life. She knew he'd had many children and he told her about the son and daughter who'd lived to adulthood but had then tragically died. He seemed desperately sad when he spoke of his daughter, Lady Margaret, and he'd shown her a painting of the young woman that was hanging on the wall in the library. Her hair, like Annie's, was auburn. But Lady Margaret's hair was piled on her head with curls framing her face, in what had been the latest fashion several years ago.

"My darling Margaret. She was the light of my life," the Duke had said.

In autumn 1787, when Lord Henry and his wife came on their annual visit, Annie was surprised to be told that she'd be required in the laundry and kitchen. As a chambermaid, she'd expected to carry out her duties as usual. Lady Constance brought her own lady's maid and servants, so Annie hadn't imagined she'd be anywhere near the Duke's sister-in-law but neither had she thought she'd be back in the kitchen. Mrs Barrett had informed her in a voice that Annie knew better than to question. It would only be for two months and then everything would go back to normal.

On the second day of the visit, one of the maids who'd carried hot water up to Lord Henry's apartment had slopped some of the contents of the bucket over the floor. Lady Constance had slipped on the water and fallen heavily. She hadn't broken anything, merely sustained bruising but she'd been in a dreadful temper. Her maid was sent downstairs to fetch servants to take the bath away immediately and to mop up the spillage.

In the ensuing panic, one of the chambermaids pleaded with Annie to go up to the room to dry the floor while the bath was emptied.

Lady Constance sat in an upholstered chair with her leg raised on a stool watching the servants scurry about carrying out her orders. However, when she saw Annie, she stopped mid-sentence and stared.

"You! What's your name, girl?"

"Annie Sherrington, Lady Constance."

"And where do you come from, Annie Sherrington?"

"My family live in Essex, madam." The lie sprang to her lips before she'd had a chance to think. But she didn't want this woman to know she'd spent much of her life in the Foundling Hospital. Somehow, admitting that her mother had abandoned her was too painful. And, after all, the only family she'd ever known had lived in Essex.

Still, Lady Constance stared at her, and Annie was grateful to finish her task and go back to the laundry.

Once the bath had been removed from her room and the spillage had been mopped up, Lady Constance dismissed all the servants except her lady's maid, Nancy.

"That maid with the ghastly red hair..." she said.

"Yes, madam?"

"You told me that His Grace's servants gossip about one of the maids, is she the one?"

"Yes, madam. They say she entertains the Duke in his rooms."

"Really? If that is true, it would be quite disgraceful."

"Yes, madam."

"I would need to inform my husband if something scandalous were taking place under this roof..."

"Yes, madam?"

"So, I would like you to find out what you can without arousing suspicions. Can you do that?"

"Yes, madam. Certainly."

Nancy returned a little later bringing interesting news. Annie Sherrington had lied. Not about her name but about her family. She had actually been apprenticed from the Foundling Hospital and had been brought to the house by Mrs Barrett, who'd continued to favour her ever since. Interesting.

While Lady Constance understood that a young girl might be so ashamed of her unfortunate beginnings that she'd conceal any time spent in the Foundling Hospital, there was another factor to take into consideration. Annie was the image of Lady Margaret at that age. Was it possible that her niece had given birth to an illegitimate child?

If that was so, then the implications for her husband were disastrous. No, surely it couldn't be true. Her imagination was playing tricks on her.

And yet, if the girl enjoyed special favour with her brother-in-law and also with the housekeeper, that suggested something suspicious. Mrs Barrett had always doted on the spoilt brat, Lady Margaret, so she'd surely favour her daughter.

But if the child truly was His Grace's granddaughter, he was obviously reluctant to acknowledge her and tell the world that his unmarried daughter had given birth.

Lady Constance examined the information she had from all angles. His Grace was a kind man. Suppose he settled a sum on the girl? Well, even so, there was plenty of money that would eventually pass to her husband. Or was there? Could the Duke leave all the money to the child? And what of the houses and their estates? Could he leave them to the girl too? And worse – the dukedom. Could he name the chit as his heir?

Panic bubbled up inside her. She must keep a clear head. She must think.

Hadn't it been done before? Hadn't the daughter of the first Duke of Monmouth or Marlborough – yes, it was Marlborough – inherited her father's title? Could it happen nowadays? Lady Constance had no idea if such legal issues could be arranged, and it would be futile asking her husband. His interest lay in the gaming tables and at the racecourse. And, besides, his mind was not as sharp as hers. He was better educated, yes. But definitely not sharper. Her husband required guiding. And incidentally, he also needed curbing. His gambling debts of late, had been eye-watering.

Lady Constance gripped the arms of the chair until her knuckles turned white. If only she was in charge of the family finances. Instead, the elder brother who'd failed to provide a suitable heir held the title and all the wealth – although he rarely seemed to enjoy any of it. The younger brother should have inherited everything but, he was a gambler, and left to his own devices would fritter away the entire fortune.

Well, it was up to her to do something. First, she would need to make discreet enquiries at Johnson, Wendle & Short, the family solicitors. Mr Johnson was uncommonly keen on a good Madeira, and she knew from experience that it lubricated his tongue. If that didn't work, she suspected that if he was offered a sufficiently large sum of money, he could be persuaded to divulge the information she required.

And if His Grace had changed his will and settled a large sum on the brat, then Lady Constance would know she was her niece's illegitimate daughter. What then? She drummed her fingers on the table.

One thing at a time.

There were invariably ways and means.

First, she would call on Mr Johnson.

Lady Constance decided that under the circumstances, it would be acceptable for her to simply visit her brother-in-law rather than request an audience. She knocked on the door and boldly entered his apartment. He was sitting in the tiny chamber reading a book and he looked up eagerly as if he'd been expecting someone. But the smile that sprang to his lips froze and his eyebrows shot upwards in surprise and displeasure. His mouth opened in rebuke, but she held up her hand in a peremptory fashion that appeared to disarm him.

"Before you say anything, Your Grace, I apologise for the intrusion, but certain information has come to my attention and I am very concerned about your welfare."

The Duke continued to stare at her.

She carried on, "I believe you have recently made changes to your will—"

"How dare you!" The Duke rose from his chair. Standing straight, he was still an imposing sight.

Constance took a half-step backwards and then checked herself. She was fighting for her husband, and right was on her side.

"I have come to demand that you reverse those changes in favour of your brother." She kept her voice steady.

The Duke stared at her silently and she wondered if he was weighing up how much she knew. Well, she would make it easy for him, she'd tell him.

"I know that red-headed chit of a girl in the kitchen is your granddaughter. Lady Margaret's illegitimate child. And I know that you have made provision for her in your will. I demand that you change your will back. Your brother deserves to inherit all the family wealth, not some kitchen wench!"

He seemed to grow in stature as he took in a deep breath and his face contorted with rage.

She'd never seen her mild-mannered brother-in-law so furious.

With nostrils flared and his eyes glittering shards of fury, he took a step towards her.

She backed away.

Then, the Duke stopped. Colour drained from his face, and he clutched his chest. He swayed for a second then collapsed into the chair, still holding his chest. His face was grey, the eyes that had just flashed fury were now sunken, dark and afraid. He gasped for breath.

Lady Constance stood for several moments, her hands over her mouth in shock.

Suppose he should die now? That would be a disaster. Mr Johnson had let slip that changes had been made to the will but he would not be drawn on exactly what they were. She rushed forward and taking his arm she led him out of the chamber and towards his bed. "I will send for a physician."

Lady Constance hurried along the corridor back to her room, muttering to herself. For years she'd looked forward to this time. Not that he was dead yet. But he must surely be close. However, now there was the complication of the red-haired girl, and the Duke's demise might well prove to be a disaster. He must not die before he'd reversed the changes in his will.

"Nancy? Where are you, girl?" Lady Constance collapsed into a chair in her room, gasping for breath.

"H...here, madam." Nancy licked her lips nervously.

"I need you to send for Dr Ibbotson on a matter of great urgency."

"Are you unwell, madam?"

"No. Yes. That is, if anyone asks, you are calling the physician for me. But when he arrives, you must take him to His Grace's room. Is that clear?"

"Yes, madam. Should I send one of His Grace's servants to him?"

"No! We wouldn't want to cause any panic at this stage. I suspect His Grace simply has indigestion, but we shall keep that to ourselves, will we not?"

"Yes, madam, if you say so."

"I do say so. And I want you to go down to the kitchen and tell Cook that I've changed my mind about today's dinner. I shall not be eating meat today. I expect fish."

There was a sharp intake of breath as Nancy anticipated Cook's response to this information.

Lady Constance took pity on her. "Simply tell Cook that I am feeling slightly indisposed, and that meat will be too heavy for me today. If she complains, tell her that I am perfectly happy to discuss the issue with her. And if anyone is rude to you, they will have to give account of themselves to me."

That should keep everyone downstairs spinning and prevent anyone from coming upstairs and poking their nose in until Dr Ibbotson arrived. In the meantime, she needed to keep calm and consider all eventualities. Finally, she nodded her head approvingly. There was nothing she could do for His Grace. The doctor would deal with him.

Mrs Barrett slid the tiny, silver box across her desk towards Annie. Annie looked at it in surprise.

"Open it," Mrs Barrett said.

Annie lifted the lid between finger and thumb. Inside, on purple velvet lay two earrings. Each contained a teardrop-shaped emerald surrounded by tiny diamonds. They were exquisite. Priceless.

"Beautiful," she said, lowering the jewellery box lid.

"Take them. They're yours."

Annie looked up sharply. Was this some kind of jest? A test of her honesty? "They're not mine." She pushed the box across the table towards the housekeeper.

Mrs Barrett steepled her fingers and rested her chin on the fingertips.

"Please, believe me, Annie, these are rightfully yours. I was going to keep them for you until your apprenticeship finished but under the current circumstances, I have no idea how much longer that is likely to be. As you know, His Grace has been taken ill and..." She paused and swallowed. "Well, suffice it to say, our positions are uncertain."

Annie knew the Duke was unwell and had deduced from the housekeeper's grave expression that it was serious.

"Your mother gave one of these as a token when she left you in the hospital and I was told that she wanted you to have the pair." Mrs Barrett kept her eyes down, avoiding Annie's gaze. She raised the lid and slid the box back across her desk.

Annie picked it up and stared at the earrings. They'd belonged to her mother? The woman who'd handed her over to strangers? Occasionally, when she'd been at the hospital, she'd caught a glimpse of a young woman clutching a baby in her arms going into the secretary's office and had wondered what sort of woman she was. Mostly, the people she'd seen had been poorly dressed and she'd assumed they couldn't afford to keep their children. But her mother? Her mother had owned a pair of emerald and diamond earrings. Money had evidently not been a problem.

45

"Do you know who my mother is?" Annie could hardly push the words out.

"The hospital would not be allowed to give that sort of information out." Mrs Barrett's cheeks reddened but she kept her eyes on the earrings. She added briskly, "We have more pressing things to consider. Since we have no idea what is going to happen to us if His Grace..." She swallowed. "Well, suffice it to say, our services may no longer be required, and we'll be asked to leave at short notice. So, there may not be time to..." She paused again and nodded at the jewellery box. "It's best you take them now and pack them in your bag, ready to leave should we all be required to go."

"But surely Lady Constance wouldn't dismiss all the staff? How would she run such a large house?"

"Indeed, she would not. But many would hand in their notice and others such as you and me would be dismissed."

"But why?"

Mrs Barrett shook her head sadly. "Suffice it to say, that's how it would be."

It wasn't until later that Annie wished she'd asked more about the earrings. Mothers usually left one token at the Foundling Hospital when they left their baby and retained the other. If someone at the hospital had given Mrs Barrett a pair, then her mother must have left two earrings. Why hadn't she kept one herself? She'd ask Mrs Barrett the next time she was alone with her although she suspected she'd just be told the hospital didn't give out that sort of information.

Despite his frail appearance, during the next few days, the Duke recovered slightly. Dr Ibbotson had prescribed bed rest, no visitors, regular bleeding which he'd undertaken each day and a tincture of foxgloves. His cures appeared to be working. Everyone within the house seemed to be holding their breath, waiting to see if His Grace would survive. Servants trod quietly as they went about their work and even Cook stopped bellowing orders. Sadly, although His Grace seemed slightly stronger, he'd lost all movement on one side and the ability to speak.

"A mere setback, that is all," said Dr Ibbotson. "His Grace simply needs time. And complete rest. Strictly no visitors."

Neither Lord Henry nor Lady Constance had been allowed to visit the Duke in his sick bed. It was just as well. Lady Constance wasn't sure she'd be able to keep silent about his will. She wondered if she should summon Mr Johnson to see His Grace anyway so he could ensure his affairs were in order. And more specifically, to prompt him to come to his senses and change his will back in favour of his younger brother. Surely the interfering physician wouldn't deny his patient access to his solicitor?

Apparently, he would.

Lady Constance was beginning to despair.

And then, a small piece of news came her way and she realised she had a perfect solution to the problem that was Annie Sherrington. Her lady's maid, Nancy, had befriended Meg, the maid who shared a bedroom with the red-headed girl. Meg had revealed that Annie had a prayer book hidden under her bed. Nothing wrong in that, of course, except Meg had looked at it and she'd noticed that the leather cover was embossed with the family coat of arms. That meant it belonged to the Duke. And the clasp was made of gold. It had obviously been stolen and if so, then Lady Constance was justified in informing the justice of the peace. Theft from one's employer was a serious offence. Annie would be removed and once found guilty, she'd be imprisoned. The value of the book would mean the death penalty. Then, when His Grace finally died, Lord Henry would inherit everything. Which is as it should have been in the first place.

But timing was important. There would be a trial and it was crucial that no one spoke up for the girl. His Grace was not well enough to appear in court. Indeed, he wasn't well enough to be informed of a theft that had taken place in his house. No, Lady Constance would ensure that was kept from him. She'd now managed to get her servants into the Duke's room, so she had more control and could keep a closer eye on things.

But Mrs Barrett... Now, there was a problem. Lady Constance knew that the housekeeper would speak up for the girl. She might even be persuasive enough to convince the court. Lady Constance couldn't take the risk.

Once again, Fate stepped in and assisted. Mrs Barrett's sister wrote to say she'd sliced her hand and the cut had become infected. Was there any way that Mrs Barrett would be able to stay with her for a week or so until she could manage again?

"Of course!" Lady Constance had said with a benevolent smile, "After all, the physician is giving the Duke the best medical attention and the house can manage for a few weeks without you. Yes, you must go as soon as possible. Furthermore, I shall order my husband's carriage to convey you to Essex with all haste. Take as long as you need."

The chief constable and his men arrived the following day, clutching a warrant that had been issued by the justice of the peace. A footman opened the door and although suspicious at first, he was soon persuaded to lead the men directly to the attic. He was then instructed to fetch Annie and Meg while a search was carried out in their room.

The two girls arrived in time to find one man crouching with his arm under Annie's mattress. He grunted with satisfaction as he pulled out a leather-bound prayer book with a golden clasp. However, of much greater interest was the small, silver jewellery box. Inside the velvet-lined box were two emerald earrings.

The constable turned to the girls with a look of mock surprise on his face, "Well, what do we have here?"

His men craned their necks to get a better view of the earrings. One of them whistled. "Worth a bit, I'd say."

"I'd say you were right, Tom," the chief constable said. "Now, which of you two is the one what sleeps in this bed?"

Annie stepped forward. "I... I can explain—"

"They all say that," said the chief constable cheerily. "And you'll have plenty of opportunity to do that to the judge. Now if you'll come along with me, miss..."

"Please sir, I can prove my innocence. If you ask Mrs Barrett, the housekeeper, she'll vouch for me. She knows the Duke gave me the prayer book and she gave me the earrings—"

"So, you're telling me that the housekeeper gave you priceless emerald and diamond earrings?"

"Yes... no... she gave them to me, but they were a gift from my mother. They were left at the Foundling Hospital for me for when I finished my apprenticeship."

The chief constable snorted in derision. "As I'm sure you're well aware, miss, His Grace isn't well enough for me to ask him and in all honesty, I wouldn't have the nerve to request an audience with him. He'd have no interest in a servant. And sadly for you, I've been informed that the housekeeper is visiting her sister in Essex and isn't due to return for several weeks. I will of course enquire at the Foundling Hospital, but I don't believe it's common practice for mothers to leave valuable items like that to be given to babies they've abandoned. Now, if you'll come along with me, miss, you'll be taken to the house of correction. It appears you need to be removed from the temptations of this house since you can't seem to keep your fingers off anything."

As the chief constable led Annie from the room, Meg looked at her feet. Her face was white and Annie guessed it had been Meg who'd gossiped about the book.

Meg's young man had run off with another girl and her bitterness had needed an outlet. Maybe she'd searched through Annie's things, looking for something to get her into trouble. Annie felt sick. For years she'd shared a room with a girl who bore her such ill will.

"I... I," Meg said as the chief constable pushed Annie past her through the door, but it wasn't clear whether she was trying to apologise. Another shove propelled Annie outside, leaving Meg's words unsaid.

As they made their way down the back stairs to the servants' entrance, on each floor servants appeared. News had travelled fast throughout the house. White faces. Open mouths. Some condemning. Some sneering. But no one with a friendly expression or with an offer of help on their lips.

But then who could help her? There were only two people in the world who could save her. Of those, one was upstairs in bed, unable to speak and too ill to disturb. And realistically, why would the Duke care about the fate of one of his maids? Even a favoured maid. The other person who Annie was sure would have helped her, was miles away in Essex.

There was still a chance that somebody at the Foundling Hospital would confirm that the earrings had been given to Mrs Barrett when she'd arranged Annie's apprenticeship.

However, it appeared that the constable was correct. The governors of the Foundling Hospital would only say that it was usual for only one token to be left by the mother but their rules on confidentiality had to be adhered to and they could be of no more help than that.

The hearing in court had lasted twelve minutes. By the time Mrs Barrett had returned from Essex, Annie had been tried, convicted – and because of the value of the items she'd been found guilty of stealing – had been sentenced to death.

Mrs Barrett begged Lady Constance to help. She knew no one else with enough influence to help although she expected her pleas to be ignored. When the ghastly woman said there was nothing she could do about a thieving maid, Mrs Barret wasn't surprised that she'd refused to help. Of course, she didn't mention Annie's relationship with His Grace and neither did Lady Constance. Did the dreadful woman know? Mrs Barrett had no idea, but she was a clever woman and if she'd ever seen Annie, she might have spotted the similarity between her and Lady

Margaret. Mrs Barrett had always insisted Annie remain in the kitchen when Lady Constance visited but it was possible she'd laid eyes on her.

When that had failed to secure Annie's release, Mrs Barrett did her best to find where Annie had been sent. She visited the justice of the peace several times, but as he pointed out on each occasion, the girl had already been sentenced. A clear message needed to be sent to the lower classes that they could not take what they wanted. An example had to be set. And what sort of example would it be if the girl was let off?

"But she's innocent. I know His Grace gave her the prayer book and I also know the child's mother left those earrings for her when she was of age." Mrs Barrett was tempted to tell the foolish man that he was talking about a duke's granddaughter, but why would he believe her? Only His Grace could confirm her story and he was unable to speak. In order to protect his daughter's memory, he might not even be willing to do that.

"Madam! Pray listen to me! It matters not that she is innocent. You are too late. She has been tried and found guilty and now she will hang." The justice of the peace arose, indicating that the meeting was over.

Mrs Barrett also rose. She placed her hands on the desk and leaned toward the man. In slow, deliberate tones, she said, "I demand that you request clemency. His Grace uttered two words this morning. If he should make a recovery or at least be able to indicate that the girl is not guilty, then I wouldn't like to be in your shoes."

"I'll see what I can do. Perhaps the sentence could be reduced to transportation..." The justice of the peace wiped his brow with his handkerchief.

Weeks after Annie had been arrested, a white-faced and dishevelled Lord Henry awoke his wife early and announced that he was in a spot of bother.

Half-awake and furious at having been disturbed, Lady Constance braced herself for news of more losses at the gaming tables. However, she was shocked to hear of the real cause of the problem. Lord Henry had just come from Hyde Park where he'd taken part in a duel.

That caught Lady Constance's attention and she sat up and took in her husband's muddy, torn breeches and stockings.

"Are you mad? You know duelling is illegal!"

Lord Henry hung his head.

"And what of your opponent?" Lady Constance added through gritted teeth, "I trust you didn't hit him?"

Lord Henry was rather vague on that point. "I think I might have caught his chin. He fell over and hit his head. His second took him away but he was still unconscious."

"So, he may yet die?" Her voice had become shrill.

"I pray not, my dear."

"You pray not?" Lady Constance sank back onto the pillows. She could feel a headache coming on. Well, there was nothing for it. They'd have to leave before the chief constable returned to question her husband. It was back to the gloom of their house in Yorkshire. She'd got used to the glamour and sparkle of London. And of course, it had been important to keep an eye on the Duke. But needs must. Yorkshire would be far enough away for Lord Henry to hide out for a while to wait and see what happened to his opponent. It might also restrict his gambling.

She looked her husband up and down. No blood that she could see. Simply muddy breeches. She suspected he'd simply dropped to his knees in fright. He really was a most irritating man.

Lady Constance pulled the silk bellpull to summon Nancy. The sooner they started packing, the sooner they could be away. On second thoughts, perhaps she and Lord Henry would leave immediately. Their luggage could follow on.

Mrs Barrett was relieved to see His Grace's brother and wife leave. She had no idea why their departure had been so abrupt, and she wasn't interested. Simply grateful that the unwelcome visitors had gone. Now she could dedicate herself to the care of the Duke. He must recover. He was Annie's only chance at being rescued. She ignored the physician's wishes and told His Grace what had been happening.

Within the week, the Duke had begun to speak. Determination burned in his eyes. Progress was slow at first, and sometimes he was frustrated when the correct word wouldn't come but he made it clear he wanted her to send for Mr Johnson, the solicitor.

"Tell Johnson everything... Margaret... Annie... Help Annie."

Mrs Barrett understood and when Mr Johnson arrived, she led him to His Grace's bedchamber and ensured he had pen and paper. His Grace nodded as she looked to him for confirmation that she should tell everything. Mrs Barrett began by explaining the history of her former mistress's child. She explained how she'd brought the girl from the Foundling Hospital to Tavistock Hall under the guise of an apprenticeship. She also said she suspected that Lady Constance had noticed the maid's resemblance to Lady Margaret and having seen how

His Grace favoured her, she'd guessed her identity. She'd also correctly guessed that the will had been changed. Mr Johnson cleared his throat several times and ran his finger around the inside of his stock as if he was having trouble breathing. Mrs Barrett didn't add that she suspected he'd been the cause of Lady Constance's 'guess'. However, she carried on while he continued taking notes and eventually, she'd told him the whole story.

Mr Johnson returned the following day with a letter he'd written on behalf of His Grace and said he'd ensure the correct people received a copy. Lord Hawkesbury as well as Sir Evan Nepean. And anyone else he thought might be able to help.

Several days later a reply came from Lord Hawkesbury saying that under the circumstances, he was confident the girl's sentence would be overturned and His Grace could rely on his discretion. However, there had been a clerical mishap and his men had so far been unable to locate the girl. It was possible that she was in transit between prison and a transport ship. But he would do his best.

However, many days passed and after no word, Mr Johnson, acting on His Grace's behalf, enquired if any progress had been made.

Lord Hawkesbury's secretary replied to say the girl had received a pardon but still had not been found. He would investigate. A reply came from Lord Hawkesbury explaining that they had finally tracked the girl down to a transport ship called the Lady Amelia. Unfortunately, it had already set sail from Portsmouth for New South Wales. The pardon would leave on the next ship bound for Sydney Cove and His Grace should rest assured that as soon as Governor Arthur Phillip received the pardon, the girl would be freed.

Mrs Barrett noted that no mention was made of the fact that Annie would be on the far side of the world, alone, and with no money for her fare home. She knew His Grace would have noticed this too. She called for Mr Johnson to come immediately. Provision must be made for Annie to be able to return home as soon as possible.

CHAPTER 9

It was low tide and Ben walked slowly along the foreshore looking down at the pebbles and the tiny curios that the Thames had washed up. Items that had been discarded over the centuries or accidentally dropped and washed away. He'd found a few coins once, but they were too worn for him to identify although he'd wanted to believe they were Roman. However, his mind wasn't on scavenging now. He was hiding. He'd had to walk a mile east of Rotherhithe so that no one from the shipyard spotted him and soon he'd have to return, but he needed time on his own to think.

To an observer, Ben's life might appear to be going well. He'd worked really hard and Mr Wilson, the master shipwright, was very pleased with him. So pleased, that a few months before, he'd suggested that if he called in a few favours, he could ensure that Ben finished his apprenticeship slightly early and could begin earning a wage.

Mr Wilson had taken to Ben from the time he'd started working with him. It was easy to see why. Ben had obeyed orders willingly and had worked exceptionally hard. He hadn't got into mischief like two of the other apprentices who'd been dismissed over the years.

Thankfully, Ben had an aptitude for working with wood and he'd loved living in the Wilson's house overlooking the Thames. There was always so much to see. Ships and vessels of all types slicing through the water – some merely crossing from one side of the river to the other, and others on their way to and from the ends of the Earth. In the shipyard where Ben worked, boats arrived for repairs, and new boats were created from wood, canvas and man's ingenuity.

At first, he'd dreamt of becoming a master shipwright like Mr Wilson and perhaps of having his own boatyard. Suspended over his yard would be a sign like Mr Wilson's but his would say B. Haywood & Co. Ltd.

At the age of fourteen, that eventuality was so far in the future, it could scarcely be believed. But now, he was over halfway through his apprenticeship, and it wouldn't be long before he'd be able to find paid employment. And if Mr Wilson was correct, he needn't even wait until he was twenty-one to complete his apprenticeship. Perhaps he could be earning wages within two years.

Furthermore, Mr Wilson had hinted that if Ben worked hard, C. Wilson & Co. might even become Wilson, Haywood & Co Shipwrights. And even more remarkably, one day, the huge shipyard in Rotherhithe would become his. That was unbelievable for a boy from the Foundling

Hospital. And yet there was a price.

Wasn't there always a price?

Ben groaned out loud and kicked at a shiny pebble, sending it spinning through the air. It fell with a splash into the shallows of the fast-flowing river and was lost. For years, he'd suppressed all thoughts of Annie. He'd written to her at the Foundling Hospital to tell her where he was when he'd first come to Rotherhithe, but he'd never received a reply. It confirmed his suspicions that she'd heard the dreadful things he'd said to Josiah and had been furious. And she'd have been right to do so – if he'd really meant those dreadful, cruel things he'd said. But surely, she'd have known that he'd never do anything to hurt her? Surely, she'd seen he was trying to protect her? Why hadn't she given him the benefit of the doubt?

Then, he'd wondered if there was another explanation for her silence. Had she caught an infection and died? He had no way of knowing. And he suspected that if he were to return to the Foundling Hospital, no one would tell him what had happened to her. They had strict regulations of secrecy, and information wouldn't be given out to him – even if he had once been a foundling himself.

If there was one thing he'd learnt since he'd left the hospital, it was that life wasn't tidy. Sometimes it flowed swiftly and surely like the waters in the Thames and at others, it swirled about in an eddy. You'd never make sense of it, you just had to ride whatever was there. He couldn't find her, so how could he make good on his promise to look after her? Anyway, perhaps by now, she was a wife. A mother. Someone who would not need him and would look on his desire to care for her with scornful anger.

So, if he'd never see Annie again, why was it so hard to imagine himself married to Rebecca Wilson? She was comely and pleasant, if a little moody. She'd made it clear that she was willing to be his wife. And her father, Charles Wilson, had also hinted that he'd be happy to welcome Ben into his family as his son-in-law. Indeed, the possibility of the apprenticeship ending slightly early which would allow him to find full-time employment was most likely to have something to do with it. In helping Ben, Mr Wilson was providing for his daughter's future. And if that was so, then the hint that at some stage in the future, the boatyard might belong to Ben, was wholly dependent upon marriage to his daughter.

Life in the Wilson's household had been strict and rigid, with a focus on hard work and moral righteousness. That was no problem to Ben who was used to following rules after his life in the hospital. Increasingly,

Rebecca had been finding excuses to spend more time with him. Out of respect to her father, he'd kept out of her way but recently, she'd made it clear she'd set her sights on him.

At first, he'd been shocked. Afraid. Suppose Mr Wilson should notice and be angry believing that he'd behaved inappropriately? But Mr Wilson had dropped hints. Indeed, he'd positively encouraged the idea.

The previous week, Ben had been invited to the theatre with the Wilson family and afterwards, to take supper with them. It had been such an honour to be invited. The following day, he realised with shame that the excitement, the rich food and the plentiful wine had turned his head. After supper, he'd found himself alone with Rebecca. She'd seized his jacket with both hands and standing on tiptoe, had kissed him. It had been a revelation. Of course, he'd known what men and women did when they were alone – he'd been aware of the act of coupling when he'd been at the Foundling Hospital – hadn't Josiah boasted of his conquests? But while he'd been under Mr Wilson's roof, he'd lived by his master's strict rules and had not spent his time pursuing any form of immorality like the other apprentices.

Rebecca had taken him completely by surprise and he hadn't expected the cascade of feelings, as shockwaves coursed through his body. He'd returned her kiss, pulling her to him and crushing her body against his. He'd only let her go when he'd heard Mrs Wilson's petticoats rustling and the tap-tap-tap of her steps as she approached. Then, common sense had taken over from instinct and he'd been appalled by what he'd done.

However, there now seemed to be an unspoken 'understanding' between the two young people – despite Ben not understanding it at all. How binding was an 'understanding'? No words had been spoken. He hadn't asked Rebecca to marry him. He hadn't even suggested it and yet, there was an undercurrent that was sweeping his feet out from beneath him.

He kicked another pebble into the river. It sank and was gone. Perhaps he should just leave? He'd made a vow to look after Annie. How could he marry another until he knew for sure that Annie didn't need him? But Annie might not want him. Round and round, his thoughts went, like a whirlpool.

He watched as a three-masted East Indiaman with billowing sails made its way to the docks. What was its cargo? Indigo, spices, tea, silk? A small rowing boat moored up on the other side of the river bobbed in its wake. For a second, he thought it had slipped its moorings but as it reached the end of the rope, it jolted to a stop and rocked wildly. It was fortunate the rope had held, or the boat would have been washed upstream and possibly been dashed to pieces when it reached London Bridge.

It was reassuring to be held securely, Ben thought. He was tied to Mr Wilson and the shipyard. And that was good. His future was assured, and he would one day be a master of his own yard if he married Rebecca. Would that be so bad?

The alternative was to cut free and go where life took him. Even if it resulted in his destruction.

Common sense said to take the safe route. But he couldn't help feeling that the rope that held him fast and kept him safe, was slowly strangling him. He stood for a while watching the bucking rowing boat gradually settle, ready to ride the wake of the next ship that passed.

The sun was beginning to sink. He'd need to hurry back to the shipyard. As he turned, it felt as though a rope was wrapping itself around his neck and chest, squeezing the life out of him. He couldn't bear it. Heading towards the sinking sun, he quickened his pace. He'd made a decision. But would his boldness trickle away when he got to the Wilson's home? He'd certainly need courage for what he had in mind.

Mr Wilson was more furious than Ben had ever seen him. Angrier by far than when he'd dismissed apprentices in the past for poor behaviour. His face turned purple, his eyes bulged and his enraged cries brought Mrs Wilson and Rebecca running. They hovered uncertainly outside, looking through the open door with huge eyes as Mr Wilson told Ben he was a selfish wretch and that he'd regret his foolish, rash decision.

"Don't bother crawling to me on your knees to give you your position back! I don't ever want to see your ungrateful face again! Gather your things and go, if that's what you want! How I could have been so foolish as to have trusted you, I'll never know."

With quaking legs, Ben climbed the stairs to the attic, packed his meagre belongings and left. Rebecca cried and begged her father to do something, but he simply told her to be silent. As Ben walked swiftly away, he dared not look back at the family with whom he'd lived for the last few years. He swallowed back tears. It wasn't that he was ungrateful, but he didn't want his life mapped out for him. He would decide his own destiny.

As he crossed London Bridge, the ropes he'd fancied he felt around his chest and neck seemed to slacken. By the time he'd got as far as Bloomsbury, the bindings were loose. He'd be his own man. But first, he had to satisfy himself that he'd tried everything to find Annie. He'd go to the Foundling Hospital and ask about her.

Ben walked into the hospital grounds. It was so familiar and yet it seemed smaller than he'd remembered. But the same sense of longing that he'd experienced as a boy returned, pulling at his insides. A feeling that something was missing, that although he'd been looked after – fed and clothed – no one had seen him for who he was. No one had cared that he'd had dreams and hopes. The blanket of warmth and safety – and love – that had been wrapped around him when he'd lived with the Trents – the couple he'd thought of as his parents – had been taken from him, leaving him feeling hollow.

Annie had understood.

As he'd suspected, no one would tell him where she'd gone after she'd left the hospital. No one would even confirm she'd been apprenticed. At the mention of her name, Matron had paused, her expression frozen, and Ben knew she'd remembered Annie. She'd immediately referred him to one of the governors who was on the premises but after his face registered recognition, he'd expressed his regrets. No information could be given out about children – current or past.

So, that was it. He'd never find Annie now.

However, as Ben made his way towards the gate, a nurse ran up behind him, glancing nervously over her shoulder. It was Harriet Feltham, who'd once been friends with Annie. She was now working in the hospital.

"If you're searching for Annie Sherrington, you've wasted your time." Her voice softened. "I'm not supposed to tell you anything, but I know how close you two were. Annie was found guilty of stealing from her employer a while ago and sentenced to death. I'm so sorry Ben." She turned swiftly on her heel and hurried back to the east wing.

Ben stared after her for several seconds. Harriet had been a good friend to Annie, so there was no reason to suspect she'd give him such dreadful news if it wasn't true. The hollow space inside him grew. Without Annie, he'd always be empty. Any remaining restraints fell away. There was nothing binding him to anyone or anything. He was completely free. Ben headed towards the docks where the merchant ships loaded and unloaded their exotic cargoes. He'd join whichever ship would take him. It didn't matter whether it was going east or west, so long as it took him far from London.

Ben joined the crew of the Royal Elizabeth and sailed west. After bringing back a cargo of sugar, rum and spices, it had sailed east, returning laden with tea and silk. On its return to London, the Royal Elizabeth had to undergo lengthy repairs and since Ben was keen to be at sea once more, he looked for another ship. He heard that the Lady Amelia was due to sail to the relatively unknown lands of New South Wales within the next few weeks.

In 1770, Captain Cook and a few other notable mariners had seen the distant shores of New South Wales and not long ago, eleven ships carrying British convicts, had arrived there. They'd first gone to Botany Bay but on discovering that it wasn't a suitable place to establish a colony, Governor Arthur Phillip had explored further and moved the fleet to Port Jackson. A new penal colony had been established in Sydney Cove and since then more convicts had been conveyed out there. However, it was a little-known part of the world. So, why shouldn't Ben sail there? After unloading the cargo of convicts, the Lady Amelia would sail for China and take on board exotic silks and spices. Perhaps tea. What would it matter what was loaded into her hold? Ben would keep on the move. Experience all the world had to offer and perhaps somewhere, he'd find something to fill the emptiness inside.

CHAPTER 10

The woman in front of Annie turned as she stepped onto the gangway; her face white with fear.

"Sam and I are here, Jane." The wind tore Annie's words from her mouth and fearing her friend hadn't heard, she reached out a reassuring hand.

A soldier prodded Jane with the butt of his musket and she stumbled forward, grabbing the rope to steady herself. Clutching it tightly with one hand, she placed the other protectively over her swollen belly. With her head lowered as if she didn't want to see where she was going, she climbed upwards towards the deck. Annie gripped the hand of the little boy, Sam, and guided him in front of her so that he could follow his mother.

Above them, sailors leaned over the sides of the ship, pointing, jeering and simply staring at the line of bedraggled women who were waiting to board. The little boy began to cry. Annie wasn't surprised; he was exhausted. The journey from London to Portsmouth on the outside of the coach had been freezing and wet. At three years of age, Sam was too young to understand what was happening. She gently pushed him forward so they could catch up with his mother.

At the top of the gangway, rough hands seized Jane and dragged her onto the deck. As soon as she'd got her balance, she pushed back through the men, trying to get to Sam. Annie had coaxed him to the top at last and she was grateful that the hands that lifted him onto the ship were kinder than they had been for the women.

Annie was seized by one shoulder and dragged onto the deck where she fell to her knees. Struggling up, she pushed her way through the crowd of women, seized Sam's hand and put her arm around Jane's shoulders.

Jane's expression was one of defeat. "I don't think I can—" The wind swallowed the rest of the sentence, but Annie knew what Jane had been about to say. Indeed, Annie didn't know how she was going to bear this voyage nor whatever lay at the end of it. But it was worse for Jane with a young child and another on the way.

When her husband had died leaving her and Sam penniless, the landlord had demanded payment of one type or another. She had no money and had rejected his advances. Spite had driven him to plant items in her room and accuse her of theft.

The two young women had met in Newgate Prison, awaiting

transportation. They'd both been found guilty and sentenced to death, but the landlord had obviously had a crisis of conscience and had begged for Jane's sentence to be commuted to transportation.

Annie had no idea why her sentence had been similarly reduced. She couldn't imagine that anyone had spoken up for her. But both of the women understood the anguish of being falsely accused and convicted, and there was now a bond between them. Annie didn't know how she'd have survived without Jane and Sam. They'd given her a reason to live. And soon there'd be another child. He or she had been the result of Jane trying to procure better food for Sam while they'd been in prison. The gaoler had demanded payment and that time, Jane had no choice. Now the baby would be born in the middle of the ocean putting its own and its mother's life at risk. What chance would it stand? Annie had promised that if anything happened to Jane, she'd look after Sam.

However hard things had got, Jane had not tried to get rid of Sam and if she and the baby survived, Annie was confident that Jane would do everything to keep her family together. Unlike Annie's mother. How different would her life have been if the woman who'd left her priceless emerald earrings had valued her enough to bring her up?

Annie recovered from seasickness faster than most of the others. Sam also recovered speedily. Jane, however, lay on her narrow cot, limp and wretched, nausea overtaking her every time she raised her head.

Annie brought Jane water and bread which she forced down. While she slept, Annie kept Sam occupied, telling him stories and taking him on deck when the prisoners were allowed to exercise.

Captain Yeats, the ship's master, appeared to be a fair man, allowing the convicts plenty of fresh air. He'd warned the women against what he'd called, 'lewdness and immorality' but with a male crew and cargo of female prisoners, he must have known that liaisons and more casual arrangements would take place. Already, the government agent, Lieutenant Brooks had taken a 'sea-wife' and others had claimed women for themselves.

Annie had no intention of trading herself in return for favours, so she kept her eyes down and avoided conversation unless it was necessary. On the prison deck, the women's beds were grouped in fours and one prisoner from each set was tasked with going on deck to bring back the rations. Since Annie had recovered from seasickness first, she'd been chosen. That had been fortunate because at least she could ensure that Jane and Sam received their food. Squabbles had already broken out on the prisoners' deck with claims that the women who were responsible for bringing food to the others had been serving up short rations.

Increasingly, Annie took over the care of Sam while Jane lay in her narrow cot. Many of the sailors treated Annie with more respect than they did the other women when they saw Sam holding her hand. The little boy's looks of wide-eyed amazement seemed to appeal to even the gruffest of sailors and several delighted in pointing out dolphins, porpoises and shoals of flying fish.

One grizzled, old sailor showed Sam how to tie knots, even giving him a small piece of cord on which to practice. It was hard to see who was enjoying the lesson most – the weather-beaten man or the young lad. What would life be like onboard without the boy? Although having Jane, Sam and the unborn baby to think about gave her reason to live, Annie wished that Jane was on land with a midwife at hand. Some of the prisoners had offered to help when Jane's time came but even if the child survived, there would still be miles to travel to the penal colony.

There was another child of a similar age to Sam on board, a little girl called Lottie but her mother and her friends were nervous of letting the little girl out of their sight and mostly it was Annie with whom Sam spent most of his time.

Tom, the leathery, old sailor who'd shown Sam how to tie simple knots, told them that within a day or so, the Lady Amelia would drop anchor in Santa Cruz.

"Where's that?" Sam asked.

Tom scratched his chin with the stem of his pipe. "Why, bless ye, lad! It's in Tenerife, an island off the coast of Africa."

"Are we nearly at Sydney?"

Tom grinned, displaying blackened, broken teeth. "Not nearly there yet, lad. 'Twill be months yet."

Sam's face fell.

"But I hear tell that Cap'n Yeats might let the..." Tom considered how best to continue, considering he was speaking to a child, "er, the ladies of the ship go ashore one evening."

Sam's eyes lit up and Annie was excited.

Oh, to walk on solid ground again! But Annie doubted that Jane would be strong enough to go ashore, even if what Tom said was true. She wondered if Jane would trust her enough to take Sam if she was allowed to go. The chance of seeing a foreign country and walking on its shores was frightening but exhilarating.

However, before they arrived at Santa Cruz, several of the prisoners started a fight and the captain ordered the ringleaders to be put in irons.

As a deterrent to such outrageous behaviour occurring on the Lady Amelia again, he'd banned the others from leaving the ship when they docked.

"Will we stop again before we get to Sydney?" Sam asked Tom as he watched him whittling a piece of wood.

"San Sebastian next."

"What's that?"

"San Sebastian de Rio de Janeiro, lad. On the coast of Brazil."

"How long before we get there?"

"Weeks yet."

"Weeks?" Sam echoed sadly. "How do you know, Tom?"

"I knows, that's all." Tom spat into the wind, looked up at the billowing sails and gave a knowing nod. Then, with a tooth-gapped grin and a wink, he added, "I knows because I've been there afore, lad!"

"Weeks," Sam said with resignation.

"But there'll be plenty of excitement afore that. About three weeks or so from Santa Cruz, we'll cross the Line."

At the mention of excitement, Sam's eyes lit up, but they soon dimmed. Crossing a line didn't sound very interesting.

"D'ye know how to tell when you're in the bottom half of the world, lad?" Tom held up the wood he'd been whittling into a spoon and inspected it.

"Bottom half?"

"The world's round, just like a ball." Tom looked around for something of a similar shape and seeing nothing, he held up the spoon by the handle. "Imagine this is England up here." He pointed to the top of the underside of the bowl. "Tenerife is about here and San Sebastian is down there. Now, if you imagine a line like this." He scored a line across the bowl of the spoon with the tip of his knife, leaving a faint scratch mark. That's the Line. There's some as call it the Equator."

Tom had aroused Sam's interest. "What happens when we go over the Line? Will we tip over?"

"Why, bless ye, lad. What happens is we have a party."

Sam jumped up and stood on a box to look over the gunwale at the horizon. "How will we know when we get there?"

Tom chuckled. "Oh, there won't be no doubt when we cross the Line. You'll see."

Tom had been correct. On the day the Lady Amelia crossed the Equator, the entire atmosphere of the ship changed. At mid-morning, the convicts were led up on deck with crowds of sailors and marines, who jostled and shouted. Soon the reason for their hilarity became apparent as the bosun climbed onto a large crate. He was dressed in a loin cloth, with a long, false beard and a crown on top of a wig made from rope strands. Brandishing a trident, he announced he was King Neptune, risen from the ocean, and then leaned forward to offer his hand to his 'wife', Queen Amphitrite.

"Or as I call her, Mrs Neptune," the bosun bellowed to the delight of the crowd. He dragged a sailor who was dressed as a woman, with a rope wig on her head, onto the crate from where the couple held court.

It was a comical ceremony and after the sailors who'd never crossed the Line before had been ducked in a large pool of seawater on the main deck, the music began. Captain Yeats allowed the women to remain on deck with the crew, and dancing and singing lasted long into the night. Even Jane managed to struggle up from the prison deck and sat on a barrel, watching the festivities. Annie hoisted Sam onto the barrel and held him steady so he could see Neptune and his queen. She remained beside Jane, happy to watch but not wanting to be part of the festivities.

When Jane said she was tired and wanted to go below to the prison deck, it was Sam who wanted to stay up longer, not Annie. Although she wasn't tired, she didn't want to remain on deck on her own. Many of the sailors and marines were drunk – as were the women – and a riotous time was being had by all. Men led women away out of the dancing throng, and it didn't need much imagination to guess what they'd be up to.

"Fools!" Jane held her hand on her belly. "A night of wantonness. And then quite probably, a price to pay."

She was right, of course. If the going was slow, it was possible that in nine months they'd still be at sea. But a little voice inside Annie whispered, *but who knows how much longer you have left on this Earth? Enjoy yourself while you can.*

That was another way of looking at things. Pay tomorrow for what you do today. But she was already paying with her future for something she hadn't done. *Why put yourself in danger unnecessarily?* The risk would have to be worth more than a drunken evening with a lowly sailor.

Why? The tiny voice asked her, *What do you think is so special about you?*

Annie couldn't answer but there seemed to be a divide between throwing herself with unthinking abandon into anything, and not caring about the outcome – like so many of her fellow prisoners – and wanting to take her time about making choices. One thing of which she was certain – the gaping emptiness inside wouldn't be filled by a night with a drunken sailor.

The following morning, Annie fetched food for Jane and Sam at the usual time. After the revelry of the previous night, many of the women were slow to get up and unusually, Sam didn't want to accompany Annie on her walk around the ship.

Up on deck, the sun had barely risen, yet it was already hot. The air was humid and still, heralding another sweltering day.

Annie looked over the gunwale, down into the water that foamed around the hull. The previous night, she, Sam and Jane had stood on the same spot and watched as the sea had lit up blue and green, seemingly from below.

Tom came up behind her. "Did ye see the colours in the sea last night?"

Annie nodded.

"The fire in the sea. All gone now. Only happens at night as far as I know. I've seen it a few times. Mermaids under the water with lamps that light up the water."

"But why doesn't the flame go out?"

"Mermaids don't use the same sort of flame." Tom clamped the stem of his pipe between his remaining teeth. "Next stop, San Sebastian. Unless we meet a disaster first."

"Is that likely?"

"Who can say?" He pointed out a shark that was swimming alongside. "The world's a surprising place. Ye never knows from one moment to the next what's likely to 'appen."

Ben walked swiftly along the main deck, his toolbox under one arm and his caulking mallet in his hand. He'd just inspected the depth of water in the bilges, and it was higher than he'd expected. Ship's carpenter, Caleb Bramwell wouldn't be happy. And today, it would mean a lot of work making the timbers of the hull watertight.

The previous day, the carpenter's mate, Arthur Towler, had assured Mr Bramwell that the area Ben had just inspected was sound. It wasn't surprising. Towler was an unpleasant, lazy man. During the Crossing the Line ceremony, he probably hadn't even gone below to look. Towler was the carpenter's mate and Ben was an assistant but increasingly, Mr Bramwell relied on Ben's judgement and work.

Several complaints had been made against Towler who was as unpopular with the Lady Amelia's crew as he was with the women on board.

A vicious, spiteful man who delighted in bearing grudges.

Ben was careful not to annoy him.

On the other hand, he didn't want to anger Mr Bramwell either, so he wasn't looking forward to delivering the bad news about the state of the hull. Usually, the carpenter would have undertaken the inspection himself, but he'd drunk himself into a stupor the previous night and had not quite come around.

Ben had enjoyed the Crossing the Line ceremony but hadn't taken part in the dancing. He had no wish to have anything to do with any of the convict women. So far, he'd managed to keep out of their way. After he'd first gone to sea, he'd sought comfort in women's arms when his ship had docked. But it had occurred to him that a woman was worth more than simply a night of pleasure. Furthermore, didn't he deserve to be treated as someone special and not just as a customer?

The emptiness inside him grew each time he was with a woman until he decided he was better off alone. If he kept busy and was permanently on the move across the Earth's waters, then he could forget the desolation inside. New countries, new customs and new challenges. They'd keep his mind off the part of him that had once been filled by his care for Annie. So, during the celebrations, he'd gone to his bunk and tried to sleep. Not that he'd been successful with all the noise, and coming and going of sailors.

Ben shifted the weight of the heavy toolbox and as he did, he marvelled that having allowed himself to think of Annie – something he didn't often do – he now fancied he could hear her voice.

He shook his head angrily to dismiss the notion. He could obviously hear one of the women who was still on deck after the night's festivities and his tired brain had moulded her voice to fit his memory of Annie's.

As he turned to look where the voice had come from, he dropped his caulking mallet in shock. The toolbox followed with a thunderous crash. The woman who'd been looking over the side of the ship with Tom – and who was now glaring open-mouthed at him – was Annie Sherrington.

Seconds ticked by while they continued to stare at each other.

Thoughts passed too quickly through Annie's mind to be able to process.

Her skin tingled, her breath caught in her throat.

Shock at seeing the changes in him now he was a man.

Humiliation that he'd see she was a convict.

Rage for past hurt.

Thoughts chased each other around her mind but words died in her throat.

Ben broke the silence. "Annie." One word. But she heard the anguish and wonder. The disbelief. And the love he'd once had for her – a brother for a sister.

Still, they stared at each other. Neither moved.

Annie's thoughts began to untangle. She took several steps toward him. Taking a deep breath, and staring deeply into his eyes, she slapped him hard across the cheek. Then, she walked away on unsteady legs back to the prisoner deck.

Ben crouched to pick up his tools and a slow smile spread across his face. His cheek stung. Annie had lost none of her fire and passion. Of course, he hadn't deserved that slap, but she'd believed he had. She hadn't held back, and the years obviously hadn't lessened her outrage. But now, she'd let him know how she felt. Perhaps after he'd explained that he'd tried to protect her, she'd understand. She might even forgive him. Her death sentence had obviously been commuted to transportation. She was alive and therefore, there was hope. Could they be friends again? At least while they were both confined to the Lady Amelia.

"She's a fiery one an' no mistake." Tom pointed towards the retreating figure of Annie with his pipe stem. "Wouldn't 'ave thought she 'ad it in 'er. So calm and quiet, she is with that lad o' hers. You must 'ave vexed 'er good an' proper."

"Lad?"

"Sam. He's a good lad."

Annie had a son? Well, why not? Years had passed since he'd seen her. She was a beautiful woman now. Later, when she'd calmed down, he'd look for her and find out what had happened to her over the last few years. He couldn't keep the grin from his face. Annie was alive. His Annie. Well, not his Annie yet. He'd have a lot of explaining to do, but he'd do anything to make it right between them.

However, first, he'd have to report to the ship's carpenter. There was much work to do to keep the ship watertight.

Predictably, Mr Bramwell was in a foul temper when he heard about the depth of the bilge water and the work that was needed to seal up the timbers. He had a thundering headache after the previous night and the sight of Towler set him off. The mate said that everything had been fine the day before, but Ben knew that couldn't be true. So did Mr Bramwell.

It took hours filling in the gaps between the planks with oakum and tar before Mr Bramwell was satisfied. Usually, the time would have passed agonisingly slowly for Ben, but his mind was full of Annie and her son. How soon could he see her? Would she allow him to explain? Who was the father of the boy? At that thought, it was as if someone had hit him with a caulking mallet, driving the caulking iron deep into him.

CHAPTER 11

"Is all well?" Jane asked when Annie returned to the prison deck.

Annie wondered whether to keep quiet about Ben and then decided against it. She wouldn't be able to conceal her agitation and Jane would guess she was hiding something.

"Yes, I've met an old friend. He's one of the crew."

Jane groaned. "Be careful, Annie."

"Yes, of course. He's someone from my childhood. He was like a brother. We grew up together, although we don't share blood."

"If red blood runs through his veins, be careful," Jane said wearily.

Later, when Annie went to fetch supper, Ben was waiting for her on the main deck.

"Can I see you tonight, Annie? Can we talk? I'd like to explain..."

"I'm not allowed out of the prison deck at night."

"But would you come if you were?"

She pressed her lips together, wanting to hurt him by refusing. But she needed to hear his explanation. "Yes."

"Then I'll pay the guard to let you out."

Annie knew bribery took place regularly as women came and went through the night, but she'd never thought she'd be one of those women.

"I'll look after you," he said guessing her thoughts. "I'd never let anyone hurt you. Please give me a chance to explain..."

Curiosity overcame her caution and she nodded.

She waited for the bell as he'd instructed and then silently made her way to the hatchway where the marine stood guard.

"Annie Sherrington," she whispered and silently he let her out. Her blood pounded in her ears. Suppose Ben had been delayed or worse – suppose he didn't come? But before she'd taken a few steps, he was there.

He led her into the shadows, and they sat down in a space between two crates. Side-by-side on the warm planks of the deck, their backs against the bulwark and their legs stretched out in front of them. Squashed together within the confined space, Annie's arm pressed against his. How comforting it was, to feel his warmth.

"Thank you for allowing me a chance to explain." He drew in a ragged breath and began to tell her how he'd tried to protect her from the attentions of Josiah.

"I thought he was your friend like Oliver Wills had been. I thought Josiah looked after you." A great weight pressed down inside Annie.

Josiah and the other boys had taunted Ben, making his life miserable and she'd been completely unaware. And worse, Ben had tried to protect her, and she'd assumed he was boasting to his friends. Why hadn't she trusted him and believed he was doing as he'd always done – protecting her?

"I'm so ashamed." Annie buried her face in her hands, one of which tingled with the memory of having slapped his cheek earlier in full view of his fellow crew members. How humiliating that must have been for him.

Ben half-turned and in the small space, awkwardly put his arm around her shoulders. "How could you have known? We were young and unprepared for life." He pulled her tight and rested his head on hers. "So, will you tell me what happened to you after that?"

Annie told him how she'd been apprenticed to the housekeeper of Tavistock Hall and how the other servants had been jealous at what they saw as preferential treatment. "His Grace said he liked the sound of my voice when I read but I still don't understand why he chose me. I didn't read any better than anyone else. If he hadn't favoured me with that prayer book and if Mrs Barrett had waited until my apprenticeship was finished to give me those earrings, I might have been there still."

Both were silent for several moments listening to the ocean lapping against the hull and the desultory slap of canvas above them.

"So, if your mother left you emerald and diamond earrings, she clearly wasn't poor?"

Annie shook her head. "It seems not."

"But she gave you away. How different would our lives have been if our mothers had kept us?"

"Who's to say our lives would have worked out any better?"

"One thing's certain, if they hadn't left us in the Foundling Hospital, we'd never have met." Ben's arm tightened around her shoulders, and she knew he was picturing her absence from his life as she was imagining his. Her mother had never been there, so how could she miss her? But Ben – he'd once been part of her.

"And what more of your life?" Ben's voice was strained, and she knew in the darkness that he was staring straight ahead as if he dared not look at her.

"That's all there is to tell."

Ben sighed and pulled away slightly. "But you have a son." He sounded disappointed.

Because he thought she had a son? Or because he thought she'd lied? For a second Annie's fury bubbled up. How dare he distrust her word?

But isn't that exactly what you once did? Hardening your heart and holding a grudge for so many years.

Annie's anger died and instead, she grasped the hand that was now on her shoulder.

"Sam is not my son. His mother is my friend and I look after him. I did not have a man during that time and neither did I want anyone. I have been totally honest with you as I always was."

He sighed and she realised he'd been holding his breath.

"Would it have mattered to you if Sam had been my son?"

Ben was silent for a few seconds. "No. No one can change whatever has happened before. But as you've been honest with me, I'll now be so with you. I couldn't bear the thought of you with a man."

Annie felt his hand tense beneath hers. "Because you feel like a protective brother?"

"Yes. No... I'm not sure. My feelings are confused. It must be the shock of finding you again after believing you dead. Yes, perhaps I'm behaving like a protective brother."

But Annie didn't think he sounded certain. She understood. His thumb was idly stroking her hand and the feelings that coursed through her were not those that a sister would feel at the touch of a brother.

Memories of that last afternoon they'd spent on Trent Farm danced in her mind like the dappled sunlight beneath the tree where they'd played. The feeling as she and Ben stood back-to-back with their arms linked through each other's, holding on to the other tightly as if they were one being. That had been a special moment. Annie and Ben joined together against the world.

Now, in her mind, she imagined them as adults linked together as one. But the image didn't feel quite right, and she realised that what she really wanted wasn't for them to be back-to-back but face-to-face, chest-to-chest, with their arms locked tightly around each other.

During the next few days as they crossed the South Atlantic, heading towards Rio de Janeiro, Annie recognised that her feelings towards Ben were definitely not those of a sister. She loved him completely as a woman loves a man.

It was hard to know what he thought of her. Her earlier vow to Ben to be completely honest with him was pushed to one side. This was too difficult to speak about. Would he be horrified if he knew the girl he thought of as his sister now loved him and longed to be in his arms? If he felt the same about her, he didn't show it, but she was aware that having upset her before, he was treading warily.

On board the ship, the temperatures soared, and the humidity increased as they sailed south. They encountered calm conditions on oily seas, interspersed by squally, tropical storms that drenched anyone on deck to the skin. There'd been a few occasions when it had been too stormy for Annie and Ben to meet but mostly, if the weather was bad, they'd managed to find somewhere sheltered to hide and spend time together.

One calm, clear night when they met on deck, Ben announced that if the southeast trade winds continued to blow, it was likely the following day that they'd reach Rio de Janeiro. And if none of the convicts misbehaved like they had before they'd arrived in Santa Cruz, Captain Yeats had said he'd allow the women ashore for the evening. Overall, the captain was pleased with the way the convicts had behaved and after all, only a fool would try to escape. An English-speaking woman who was unaware of the local customs would not be able to hide easily in a place where Portuguese was spoken and where life was very different. Any escapees would soon be returned to the ship, and Captain Yeats had promised the punishment would be severe.

Shortly after noon the following day, the lookout spied the shores of Brazil and even Jane struggled up the ladder from below to join the others on deck to see their first sight of land for weeks. Gaol fever had broken out on the prison deck and there were cases of scurvy too. Fresh supplies of food and water were desperately needed so land was a welcome sight.

Jane had no intention of getting off the ship nor of allowing Sam to accompany Annie when she went ashore.

"And if I were you, I wouldn't go either." Jane regarded Annie with a sorrowful expression.

But Annie was too excited at the prospect of spending an evening ashore with Ben. An entire evening! Not just a few minutes snatched here and there.

Longboats carried the women to the shore and Ben was there waiting for her. He took her arm, and she glanced down at her dowdy, grey-striped prison garb, ashamed on his behalf. But Ben didn't seem to notice. In fact, he was looking at her with such admiration, she could have been a duchess dressed in finest silks.

He took her arm and led her away from the harbour to one of the main streets. She hadn't expected such a blaze of colour. People dressed in bright clothes promenaded along the paved streets. Many stopped at the corners to observe images and statues of the Virgin Mary and to leave offerings of exotic blooms there. The babble of Portuguese filled the air that was heavy with aromatic spices and the fragrance of flowers. Annie held on to Ben with both hands, afraid of being separated from him in the throng. A religious procession, headed by men bearing the statue of a saint and others beating drums and chanting to the beat, filled the square ahead of them. Ben held her back to allow the crowd through while petals rained down from the balconies and windows above.

"Let's find somewhere quieter," Ben said when the procession had passed. They stopped to eat sardines that had been skewered and grilled over a fire by a street vendor. Then, Ben bought pastries dripping with honey from another seller.

"Where are we going?" Annie asked as he led her towards the harbour. She licked her fingers clean and took his arm again. "Do we have to go back now?"

Ben shook his head. "No, the longboats won't leave for the ship yet. I wanted to find a quiet square where we could talk... but perhaps you'd prefer to follow the music and find somewhere lively?"

Annie shook her head. She was happy to be by his side with her arm tucked into his, it wasn't the same as when they'd stood back-to-back and linked arms as children – it was better – it bound him to her and made her feel secure. At least they were heading in the same direction. Together.

Walking away from the revelry and laughter, they found a square lit by a lantern in the centre. Next to it, a small fountain played; its water tinkling and adding to the distant music and rhythmic call of unseen insects that filled the night air. Ben led her to a bench at the edge of the square. It was set in a bower over which foliage grew, dotted with large flowers. During the day it would have provided welcome shade, but the sun had long since dipped below the hills and it now offered deep, fragrant shadow.

They sat down but still, he held onto her arm. With his free hand, he rummaged in his pocket and withdrew something which he held up.

The lantern gave enough light for Annie to see a small disc suspended on a red ribbon, spinning. He handed it to her and when she saw the polished faces of the disc were engraved, she allowed the lantern light to skim first one side, then the other. On each was engraved a heart inside which was a number. Her Foundling Hospital number on one side and his on the other. Warmth radiated through her body. No one had ever given her anything so precious. Of course, she'd once briefly owned emerald earrings and they'd been worth a fortune. But in her eyes, they had no value at all. Not like this wooden replica of the metal tokens that she and Ben had worn as babies and young children. Tears sprang to her eyes as she held it up by the ribbon and watched the disc twirl.

"I made one for you years ago when I knew I was about to be apprenticed so you wouldn't forget me... but it was the night that..." Ben fell silent, and she gave his hand a reassuring squeeze to let him know that night was to be forgotten and that she now understood. More than that, she loved him for caring so much that he'd risked taking a beating for her. However, a squeeze of the hand would not convey that message, she knew.

"But I dropped it," he said, "as far as I know, it's still there or more likely it's rotted away. I also had a flower for you." He reached out to the vine under which they were sitting and plucked a flower. He held it out to her.

"It was nowhere near as beautiful as that. I picked it in the vegetable garden."

The lump in her throat grew larger. All those years ago, Ben had thought enough of her to have made her a gift and to have thought to pick her a flower. He'd tried to protect her. And now, he was trying to make up for a misunderstanding that had been of her making. As she lifted the bloom to her nose and breathed in the heady scent, she hastily wiped away a tear. She closed her eyes and tried to find a place in her memory where she could hold this moment. The sounds, the smell and the knowledge that she was valued. It would have to last for the next seven years while she served her sentence.

They were both silent. Was he, like her, wondering what life would have been like had Josiah not followed him that day? Would it have made any difference to the events that had unfolded? Probably not but at least they'd have known that somewhere in London, also serving an apprenticeship, was someone who cared. And that one day in the future, they'd be able to meet again.

"See, I have one too," Ben broke the silence. Tucking his finger inside the neck of his shirt, he looped it around the ribbon and pulled out a disc similar to Annie's. "Our two numbers always side-by-side."

"Back-to-back, you mean." She smiled and reminded him of the memories she had of them swinging each other up in the air on that far-off day in an Essex meadow. "I loved that game. But now," she said stroking his hand, "it's even better to know you're actually by my side."

Ben allowed the disc to fall and hang by its ribbon against his chest. After a moment's hesitation, he put his fingertips on her shoulder and drew her around so she was facing him, their noses inches apart.

She could hear his breath, ragged and shallow, matching the rhythm of hers, and his hand on her shoulder trembled slightly.

He swallowed. "I wanted to ask you if you think of me as a brother. Because if you do, then I will stop now..."

"Stop?" Her voice was a hoarse whisper. What was he about to start? But as she uttered the word, he sprang away.

"I beg your pardon. I would never hurt you. You know that don't you?" His face was a mask of confusion and shame. "I understand if you only think of me as a brother. I will respect that. But during the last few days, I've been giving things much thought. We are not blood-related, so not truly brother and sister. And now, I... I feel differently about you. I feel about you like a man feels about a woman."

She was aware that he was holding his breath.

So many words leapt into her mind. 'I feel the same way about you,' 'I love you but not as a brother,', 'Please hold me.' But all that came out of her mouth was "Ben..."

He stood up and moved away from her "I'll respect your wishes. Please forget my words."

Annie leapt up and threw her arms around his neck. Her mind was full of words that refused to come out in a sensible order. Well, if her mouth wouldn't form the right words, then she'd use it to demonstrate to Ben how she felt. As she placed her lips on his, he froze and the thought that she'd somehow misunderstood what he'd meant sliced into her. She stopped. But before she could pull away, his body softened, melting into hers and his lips responded to her kiss.

Once, with angled arms and rigid backs, they'd clung to each other, swinging each other up in the air. Now, their bodies were warm and flowing, as if they'd been poured into a mould together.

Ben cupped her face in his hands, gently breaking away from their kiss. He gazed at her intently. "If you have any doubts about us being together, please tell me now."

Annie shook her head. "There's no doubt in my mind that I want to be with you, but it isn't going to be possible."

He rested his forehead on hers. "I'll wait for as long as it takes for us to be together. I promise. I'll make arrangements to stay in Sydney. I'll find work. I can build houses or ships, whatever's needed and then one day when you're free, we'll go home, and together, we'll prove your innocence."

Ben's eyes shone with fierce determination. It was tempting to believe that his heartfelt words and the strong arms wrapped around her would make everything right. And why shouldn't they? The only part of her life that had been pleasurable had been the first few years that had been shared with Ben. Once they'd been torn apart, everything had gone wrong. Now they were back together, surely things would improve?

Nevertheless, disappointment had haunted her for too many years for her to trust that Fate would grant her happiness. Something icy trickled down her spine making her shiver with fear.

"Hold me and kiss me again," Annie whispered and pressed her lips to Ben's.

If Fate didn't favour her, she wanted to remember this evening. The spicy, floral tones that drifted on the warm breeze, the humming and chirruping of the insects, the trail of pleasure left by Ben's hands as they explored her body and the sweet honey taste of his lips.

Annie and Ben wandered slowly to the harbour and the longboats waiting to take them back to the ship. The Lady Amelia would remain at anchor for a few more days while supplies were loaded ready for the next leg of the journey to Cape Town. After that, the next stop would be their final destination – if the ship survived the rough seas of the Roaring Forties.

Annie and Ben met on deck when they could. However, when the Lady Amelia arrived in Cape Town, Ben was needed on board to carry out urgent repairs and although the women were allowed ashore for one evening, Annie didn't want to go without Ben. Anyway, Annie didn't want to leave Jane. She'd given birth to a girl shortly after leaving Rio. She called her daughter Alice and despite the long and difficult birth, the child was thriving. Jane doted on her. The dreadful beginnings of the baby's life in the dingy London prison were forgotten and Jane was now determined that she'd do the best for her two children. Annie admired her greatly. In the future, Sam and Alice would never experience the shock of knowing their mother had given them away.

Once the repairs to the ship were complete and the provisions had been loaded ready for the next part of the voyage, the Lady Amelia sailed out of Table Bay. Two days after she'd turned into the westerly winds towards the Roaring Forties – the notorious latitudes between 40 and 50 degrees south of the Equator – a merchant vessel had limped into Table Bay and dropped anchor. The Emerald had left Portsmouth several weeks after the Lady Amelia but had sailed directly to Cape Town. Off the coast of Africa, she'd encountered a vicious storm that had damaged her mainmast and rigging and after almost sinking, she managed to make port.

Aboard the Emerald were letters and packets for Captain Yeats and his crew, as well as for officials and convicts in her next stop – Sydney Cove. She should have intercepted the Lady Amelia in Cape Town, but it couldn't be helped. Seafarers understood the vagaries of wind and tides, and no one would blame the captain of the Emerald. The ship was manoeuvrable and fast. Once she'd been repaired, she'd easily catch the much slower convict transport ship, although the Roaring Forties were always challenging.

However, the day before the Emerald was ready to weigh anchor, it suffered another disaster. The carpenter allowed a pot of pitch to boil over, starting a fire on the main deck. The flames were finally brought under control but not until they'd caused much damage to the mainsail and the mast. By the time it was ready to set sail, the Lady Amelia had a considerable lead.

Many of the letters and packets on board the Emerald were addressed to Governor Arthur Phillip, and one was from the Home Secretary, Lord Grenville, advising him that the Duke of Westervale had contacted him directly. There had been a miscarriage of justice concerning the duke's granddaughter. She was to receive a pardon and suitable passage was to be booked for her to return home as speedily as possible. Any expenses would be covered by His Grace, the Duke. The girl, Annie Sherrington, henceforth to be known as Lady Caroline, was to be treated with the respect due to the granddaughter of a duke.

CHAPTER 12

Several days passed while the Lady Amelia battled the ferocious winds and mountainous seas of the sub-Antarctic. Snow and hail forced the women to huddle below in the close atmosphere of the prison deck to keep warm. However, finally, news reached them that a lookout had sighted the perilous coast of Van Diemen's Land.

Annie went on deck to meet Ben and they huddled together, trying to keep each other warm while they watched the snow-topped hills of this strange, new land. Along the distant shores, far-off bonfires flashed and flared and Annie wondered if the natives she'd heard about were welcoming the ship or warning it away. Perhaps they were carrying on with their mysterious lives, ignoring the ship.

The Lady Amelia rounded the tip of Van Diemen's Land and then began to sail in a northerly direction, away from the freezing waters and bone-chilling winds. Day by day, the breeze grew warmer and eventually, the ship reached the heads of Port Jackson, which marked the entrance to the waters containing Sydney Cove.

Women gathered on the deck and regarded the sandy-coloured outcrops, the stretches of beach and the wild, tangled vegetation that came to an abrupt halt at the water's edge. This land was nothing like the gentle, green shores they'd left all those months ago. Here, the sun shone in a startlingly blue sky, with a light that was brighter, harsher and more dazzling in its intensity than any they'd ever seen before. The trees and foliage didn't have the familiar shapes of those they'd known in England, nor were they lush green. Many of the trees were tall and angular, with white, bark-draped trunks and muted grey-green or silver leaves.

The air was filled with the startling cries of unfamiliar birds and every so often, the call of something unseen rang out from the dense undergrowth. But more alarming than the sound of hidden creatures, was the occasional glimpse of a dark figure at the water's edge. A solid person or a man-shaped shadow – it was hard to tell which – that disappeared into the depths of the dense forest as soon as it appeared.

So, this was it. New South Wales, the land where Annie would spend the next seven years of her life – assuming she survived that long. She'd climbed the ladder for the last time to the main deck and looked back with longing at the dark, stinking, damp and hated place that had been her home for the best part of a year. The familiarity of the cramped quarters tugging at her, its discomfort forgotten in the face of the unknown that was a short boat ride away.

The women and their meagre belongings were loaded into the longboats ready to be conveyed to the shore. Panic, fear, resignation or determination could be seen on the faces of the women sitting around Annie, clutching bags or children to their breasts. Even the most boisterous among them was quiet.

Annie looked up at the sailors who were leaning over the gunwale of the Lady Amelia, and searched for Ben's face. Several of them watched the departing boats holding out a hand as if to touch the women they'd grown to love.

Many waved merrily to the ones with whom they'd spent much of the voyage. Their faces showed sadness, but Annie suspected the convict women would soon be forgotten, and easily replaced in the next port.

Others simply looked down with relief as the sailors in the longboats began to row the convict women away. As soon as the ship had re-stocked with supplies and water, the journey to China would be much quieter and less complicated.

Annie spotted Arthur Towler further along the deck, his cruel face twisted in a scowl. An involuntary shiver of revulsion rippled through her body. He was a disgusting man who'd been flogged on several occasions during the voyage for a range of misdemeanours. He'd started various drunken brawls, had mistreated several of the women and had tried to get Ben into trouble with the ship's carpenter. Captain Yeats was a lenient master who reserved flogging for the most serious misdemeanours but Ben had explained to Annie that in order to maintain discipline, he sometimes had to make an example of someone. Towler had often been that 'someone'.

Her eyes moved on, skimming the faces for Ben. Where was he? Finally, she spotted him, elbowing his way through the sailors until he got to the gunwale. With both hands extended towards her, he leaned forwards, his face full of longing and love. Tears stung her eyes and she put her hand over her mouth to hold back the sobs. The other, she extended towards him.

The ship's carpenter had insisted Ben remain on board until all the repairs had been completed and the ship made watertight again. The last few weeks of dreadful conditions had caused much damage. Towler was leaving the ship at Sidney to start a new life and he was due to depart after the longboats returned.

As soon as Mr Bramwell was satisfied the ship was ready to sail for China, Ben would ask to be released from the papers he'd signed that required him to remain on the Lady Amelia until the end of its voyage. Captain Yeats was a reasonable man – he'd surely allow Ben to remain in Sydney.

There was panic at the quayside when the longboats arrived. Several of the women who hadn't disembarked at Rio or Cape Town climbed out of the boats to discover the rocking motion they'd come to accept as normal, had stopped. One collapsed to her knees. The sights, sounds and smells of this new country were worrying enough without the ground that looked as though it was solid beneath their feet, seeming to ripple and roll. Ben had explained to Annie when they'd docked in Rio about the strange swaying sensation that she'd feel after time spent at sea. It was most disconcerting, but she knew it would pass. It was most likely that many others were suffering from scurvy as well and were weak from inactivity.

Annie, too, had the tell-tale bruises and the metallic taste of blood in her mouth that showed she was suffering the symptoms of scurvy. It was Ben who'd recognised the signs. He'd insisted she saw the ship's surgeon who'd given her a dose of essence of malt but even so, fresh food would be necessary before the symptoms disappeared completely.

The anxious women were herded into groups according to name. Jane, holding Alice tightly in one arm and Sam by the hand, was pushed by a burly, red-coated marine into a group that was led away, while Annie was left behind. There had been no time to say goodbye. She shouted to Jane but her voice was swallowed by the uproar.

A marine jabbed Annie with the butt of his musket, shoving her towards a group of women. She lost sight of Jane and the children as she was herded away towards the women's camp. Marines divided the remaining women into groups of four and allotted bark huts to each group.

"That ain't gonna keep out the wet," the tallest of Annie's group said surveying the thatched roof and then the leaden clouds that were rolling across the sky towards them. But the rain held off until after the women had been lined up on the parade ground and Governor Arthur Phillip had addressed them. He told them of his vision for the future of the colony but warned them the punishment would be severe for anyone committing a crime. He looked meaningfully at the steel triangle at the side of the parade ground to which offenders would be strapped before they were flogged. Harvests were so unreliable in the colony that theft of food – whether from a free man or a convict, was taken so seriously, it would be punished by death. He told them that most of the women would be moved to their new homes during the following few days and if they knew what was good for them, they'd work hard and keep out of trouble.

As thunder grumbled in the distance and jagged streaks of lightning flashed across black, roiling clouds, the women were led back to their huts.

"Huzzah!" the tallest girl said, her lip curled in scorn. "Home sweet home."

No one replied. The following day, they'd be moved on. And then who knew what might happen?

The next morning, Annie rose when the bugle sounded. The storm had raged for hours, shaking the ground when it had passed overhead, and rain had dripped relentlessly through the thatch most of the night. No one had slept well, and the women were subdued.

The oldest and weakest of the women were told they'd be set to sewing 'slops' – the clothes worn by the convicts – and were guided away. Annie kept a look out for Jane, hoping they'd be together but there was no sign of her or the children.

The younger, healthier women were told they'd work in service or on the land. Some would go to the government farms and others to convicts who'd been granted a ticket-of-leave and were entitled to convict labour to help them on their farms. With the threat of crop failure ever present, food production in the colony was vital.

Eli Evans' farm consisted of several acres to the east of Sydney Town.

"I'll take that one," he said pointing at Annie, his deeply lined face betraying a man who rarely laughed and often found fault. A marine officer made a note of where Annie would be going, and he nodded his head that she should go with the farmer.

Annie followed Mr Evans to a cart which was loaded with timber. He grunted and jerked his head to indicate she should climb up in the back. The journey was uncomfortable on the rough wood as the cart juddered over the rutted track. Men and women were working in the fields that flanked the road, and from her elevated position, to her left, she could see the sparkle of the ocean. Ben wasn't far away. What was he doing now? Had he finished the ship's repairs? How long before she could see him?

When the cart pulled up in front of a wooden cabin, a woman came out wiping her hands on her apron.

"That's Mrs Evans." Mr Evans nodded his head towards his wife without a smile. "Do as she tells you or yer'll have me to answer to."

Thin wisps of hair escaped from beneath the woman's cap and dangled lifelessly around her impassive face. She didn't acknowledge Annie until her husband had whistled for his dogs and disappeared into the barn.

"What's yer name, dear?" She spoke quietly as if the effort was too much for her.

"Annie Sherrington."

"Well, Annie. Do as Mr Evans tells yer and yer'll be fine." Her smile was wan and mournful.

Annie guessed Mrs Evans was about the same age as her but she had the appearance of one who'd experienced a hard life that had only delivered setbacks and disappointments. Would Annie look like that one day or would her luck finally turn? It all depended on Ben.

"Yer'd best follow me," Mrs Evans said.

Annie quickly followed.

It was Ben who'd first spotted that one of the masts had developed a small crack. Mr Bramwell had climbed aloft to the main yard when he'd slipped. It had been fortunate he hadn't been killed. The unconscious Mr Bramwell was carried down to Surgeon Dawson's tiny hospital and Ben sat with him until he regained consciousness.

"Well, I won't be climbing any masts for a while, that's for sure. Don't look so glum, lad. With Towler gone, I'll recommend to Captain Yeats that he promotes you until I'm up and about."

"B...but as soon as all the repairs were done, I was going to ask you if you'd put in a good word to the captain, so he'd release me from my contract."

Mr Bramwell shook his head and winced as pain shot through him. "I'm sorry, lad, I would've gladly, if I hadn't fallen. But we can't spare you now. It's not just the repairs. But the prison deck must be converted to a cargo hold ready for our arrival in China. Now, I know you've formed an attachment to that convict lassie but with me out of action, the ship needs a competent carpenter. And if you're thinking we might entice Towler to stay – think again. I don't want that scoundrel aboard any longer than he needs to be." Mr Bramwell lay back on the pillow, beads of sweat popping out on his forehead at the effort of speaking.

A bitter taste rose to Ben's throat.

How could this have happened? Was it so much to ask that just once, Fate smile on him and Annie?

"Now, I know what you're thinkin', lad." Mr Bramwell's voice was kindly. "You're thinkin' you might jump ship and take the consequences..."

Ben reddened slightly. Of course, he'd been thinking that. How could he possibly sail away and leave Annie here? It would be months before the ship returned to London and then how long until he could get passage back to Sydney? In all, it could be years...

"With any luck, I'll be well enough by the time we get to China. With your extra duties, you'll have earned more than enough to pay for passage back to Sydney to be with your lassie if that's what you want. But the women in Canton are mighty friendly. Who knows, you might find someone better. Just think about it. What d'you say, lad?"

Ben nodded. Yes, he'd think about it. But he knew he'd decide to stay in Sydney. What choice did he have?

His mind whirred. What were his options? He'd work hard and perhaps, after all, Mr Bramwell wasn't hurt as badly as it appeared. Surgeon Dawson didn't think he'd broken anything so perhaps after a few days' rest, he'd be well enough to supervise the apprentices and would be able to recommend that Captain Yeats let Ben go before the ship sailed.

In order to get the repairs to the mast completed speedily, Mr Bramwell had seen the sense in promising Arthur Towler good wages, to remain on board for a few days to assist Ben. He agreed. It wasn't clear whether this was a blessing or a curse and Ben kept out of the detestable man's way. The former carpenter's mate was not likely to take any notice of someone junior to him and Ben dreaded checking up on him as Mr Bramwell had told him to do.

Towler had already found a home ashore and he returned there each night after working all day on the Lady Amelia. He conveyed himself between ship and shore in a small rowing boat he'd acquired which meant that he didn't have to rely on the ship's longboats and could come and go as he pleased.

Thankfully, Towler seemed to work reasonably hard, and Ben was relieved that he didn't have to report him to Mr Bramwell for failing to complete his duties when he gave his daily report.

The only regrettable thing was that Towler made no effort to keep the carpenter's room tidy. Neither did he clean the tools before they were stowed back in the chests and locked away as Mr Bramwell always insisted.

When Ben told him to clean his mess away one evening, Towler laughed and walked away. "Do it yourself," being his only comment.

After the end of each long, tiring day, Ben and the apprentices tidied away the tools Towler had left lying about and swept up ready to start early the next morning. But at least gradually, they were getting all the work done.

Several of the apprentices grumbled at the extra workload and watched the sailors who had shore leave with envy. Men were going ashore as often as they could to the grog shops and the taverns and to take advantage of everything the growing town had to offer.

Some of those men who'd formed an attachment to a convict woman also searched for their loved ones and were reunited – albeit briefly. Peter Lowe, one of the sailors, had fallen in love with a convict girl and at the first opportunity, had gone ashore to find her. He'd thought himself fortunate when, within half an hour of setting foot in Sydney, he'd encountered a convict who knew his girl. She'd sent him to the house where the girl was working as a servant. But when Peter got there, he found that she'd only been there for one day. The mistress of the house had taken an instant dislike to her, and she'd been moved back into Sydney Town. From there, the trail had gone cold and eventually, in desperation, Peter had bribed a clerk in Government House. The man had been particular about pocketing the coins but not so careful in providing the correct information. He directed Peter to a farm on the east of Sydney where she was living and working with a farmer and his wife.

Peter had immediately gone there, only to find that the man had mistaken his girl Anne Shelton for Annie Sherrington. Footsore and angry, he'd returned to the office and grabbing a handful of the man's shirt, had held him against the wall and demanded to know where his girl was. He'd finally been reunited with her but now back on board, he told his story with relish, especially the last part where he'd finally extracted the information from the clerk.

Ben was overjoyed. At last, Fate was favouring them. Now, with no effort on his part, he knew where Annie was living. Before when he'd thought of her, he had no backdrop against which to place her. Was she confined to a building? A hut? A tent? Now at least he could imagine her working in a field – even if it wasn't the sort of field he was familiar with such as those he and Annie had grown up on in Essex. He closed his mind to the thought of her working out in the beating sun on this strange land that from what he'd heard, was overrun with snakes, venomous spiders and savages.

During the hours Ben spent measuring, sawing, and planing wood, his mind churned as he put together a plan. If he was set free to stay in Sydney, he'd find a job. He knew Arthur Towler planned to set himself up as a carpenter, but Ben would keep out of his way. Carpenters were always in demand and from what Peter Lowe had said, the colony was expanding rapidly with people requiring new houses and shops. There would surely be more than enough work for him and Towler. Ben would soon earn enough to keep him and Annie. He understood that as a free man, he could apply for a convict servant. If the farmer she was living with didn't want to give Annie up, he'd offer him enough until he was satisfied. Yes, it could work. He would make it work.

That night, before Towler left the ship in his tiny rowing boat, Ben asked him to help tidy away and clean the tools. The apprentices had been allowed to go ashore and Ben would be up again in a few hours to start work.

"Do it yourself! I'm the carpenter's mate. You don't tell me what to do. You do as I say."

"I would do it myself if you'd bother to bring the tools back when you'd finished with them." Ben was crouching by one of the tool chests looking for a chisel that he knew had been there the previous day. Towler lashed out with his foot, knocking Ben over.

The man was insufferable. Although Ben had previously been wary of him, now his resentment at the unprovoked kick and having to work twice as hard because of this man's shoddy workmanship, welled up inside. He leapt up and bunched his fists, ready for a fight. Towler recognised the fury in Ben's eyes and from inside his bag that lay on the workbench, he withdrew a caulking mallet and held it up, ready for an attack.

The sight of the tool stopped Ben instantly – not just because he knew Towler wouldn't hesitate to use it – but because it had been in Towler's bag. That could only mean one thing – the carpenter's mate had been about to steal it. Poised, ready to strike, Towler now followed Ben's gaze to the bag lying on the bench. The canvas draped over the contents, and it appeared that inside was a small axe.

Ben stared at him, unable to believe he was trying to steal tools. No. He'd surely brought them back to the carpenter's shop in his bag and was about to leave them out for Ben to clean and put away. But Towler's cheeks heightened in colour, and he snatched the bag to his chest, his face twisting in fury.

"You didn't see nothin'." His voice was low and menacing.

"But you can't steal tools from a ship. They might be the difference between life and death if there's damage—"

Towler sprang at Ben, pushing him against the bulkhead with one shoulder, knocking the wind from him. With his hand around Ben's neck, Towler pushed upwards and squeezed. Ben's fingers clawed at the

84

hand around his throat as he fought for breath. But Towler was desperate. The punishment for stealing tools was severe and both men knew it. He put his considerable strength into crushing Ben against the wall.

With his face inches from Ben's, he whispered, "If yer know what's good for yer, yer'll say nothing. Understand? Yer've got enough to think about now you know where your girl is. Think about that and not about making life hard for me. If you tell anyone, I'll pay your girl a visit. I know where she is; I listened when Lowe told everyone. She's with a chap called Evans. That's right, isn't it? A farm out to the east. Yes, I'll be sure to visit your girl meself once yer gone." His nose was now almost touching Ben's, and his eyes were slits. "I 'spect she'll be right glad to see a familiar face once you've sailed off. Someone needs to keep an eye on 'er. This is a dangerous country and accidents happen all the time." Towler drew back and releasing his grip on Ben's throat, he slowly drew a line across it with his finger.

"It's up to you. Keep quiet and I'll leave 'er alone. Breathe a word and the girl will pay. D'you understand?"

Ben nodded and massaged his throat. He wanted to punch the man even though he knew Towler could easily kill him.

Stepping back from Ben, Towler turned and scooped up several of the tools off the bench. He thrust them into his bag, then clutching it to his chest, he strode out of the room. "Remember, I'll make 'er pay if I 'ave to."

Ben slowly let out his breath. At least, now, there was no doubt in his mind. He would not stay aboard the Lady Amelia when she set sail for China. He'd go to Sydney and somehow find a way of being with Annie.

Guilt clawed at his insides. He couldn't risk Annie's life by telling anyone about the missing tools, but he knew what a blow it would be when Mr Bramwell discovered they'd gone. Perhaps he'd believe Ben had taken them. Well, there was nothing he could do about that.

He thumped both fists on the workbench, trying to vent his fury and as he did so, the door to the wood store swung open. Ben kicked it shut. He clenched his fists and took deep breaths. Taking out his rage on benches and doors wasn't going to help.

He sighed. Well, if he intended to stay in Sydney, then he owed it to Mr Bramwell to make sure everything was tidy – even if tools were missing. Ben opened the wood store door, checking he hadn't damaged it and looked inside. It too, was untidy. Towler had been in there earlier and had probably been looking for anything he could take away with him that would make his life easier in Sydney.

Ben put the offcuts away, sliding the longer pieces of wood into the depths of the hold, the way the carpenter had shown him.

A thought came to him. Perhaps he could make things up to Mr Bramwell and keep Annie safe. Suppose he were to smuggle her aboard and hide her in the wood store? If he could keep her concealed until they reached China, they could both jump ship when they got to Canton. It was a large port, and it wouldn't be hard for Mr Bramwell to find a new carpenter's mate and assistant. And buy more tools.

Ben would find a job and stay until they had some money saved, then he'd get work on a ship and pay for Annie's passage. Of course, they wouldn't be able to go to London because a prisoner who'd been transported and had returned to England before they'd received a pardon, would be hanged. But perhaps they could go somewhere like San Sebastian de Rio de Janeiro. They'd been happy there.

Could it work? Of course, there was a possibility that if anyone discovered Annie was a convict, she might be held by the authorities and eventually sent back to Sydney, but how would anyone find out? They'd marry and people would consider them a respectable married couple. It wasn't like she'd even committed the crime of which she'd been accused. So why should she pay? And anyway, what choice did they have? Towler was a vicious man – he'd already proved that with several of the convict women during the long voyage who still bore the scars. And before Ben had caught him stealing tools, Towler already had a grudge against him because he considered he'd turned Mr Bramwell against him. But now, the situation was even more hopeless.

Ben groaned. The plan was dangerous and desperate. Sheer stupidity. And yet the more he thought about it, the more he wondered if it was his only option. The Lady Amelia was due to set sail in two days. He had that long to contact Annie and to put his plan into action – if she agreed, of course. The repair work and alterations to the cargo deck were almost finished and the following day was Sunday. Ben would go across to Sydney for the first time. He'd find Annie and tell her of his idea, then, if she agreed he'd bring her back to the ship.

In the morning, Ben rose early. He'd gone to bed late the previous night having rearranged pieces of wood in the store. In one corner, to the left of the door, was a place deep in shadow. It wasn't immediately visible to someone who simply opened the door. That was where he'd built a false wall behind which would be a small hiding place, just large enough for Annie to lie down. He'd found some folded canvas and laid it in there to try to make the place more comfortable. Luckily, he'd also come across some old, torn clothes that someone intended to mend but appeared to have been forgotten. Ben carefully patched up the trousers and jacket. They'd be obvious under scrutiny, but Annie wouldn't be able to swim in petticoats.

Swim. Would Annie agree to such a desperate plan? He'd learn soon enough. Assuming he could find her and speak to her.

CHAPTER 13

It was Sunday and Annie had risen even earlier than usual to feed the chickens and other farm animals. To Mr Evans' dismay, and his wife's surprise, the two large, wolf-like dogs that guarded the farm took to Annie.

Mrs Evans had described them as 'demons' and had told Annie to keep as far from them as possible. She remarked that she didn't need a servant with only one hand.

"She'll do well enough. If she keeps 'erself to 'erself, she'll keep 'er 'ands." Mr Evans had replied.

But he'd been displeased when he'd seen how, after a few days, the snarling brutes wagged their tails when Annie approached them with their food. Mostly, they were tethered on long chains that would allow them to reach anyone who approached the Evans' barn without the knowledge of the farmer. Eli Evans knew all about people helping themselves to the property of others, having been convicted of stealing sheep from a farm in Shropshire. In a colony largely peopled by convicts, one couldn't be too careful, and he didn't intend to let his guard down.

He was sullen and uncommunicative, but he seemed to have the knack of farming and had somehow been successful with his crops and animals. So successful that the Governor had consulted him on two occasions about farming matters.

It was certain that others also knew of the Evans' success and might want to help themselves to a portion of it. The two unnamed dogs would soon put them right, especially if Mr Evans set them free to chase a miscreant. So, he'd found it most disturbing that they didn't display any aggression towards the convict girl.

Annie had simply spoken to them in the same way that she had to the cats in the Foundling Hospital and to the dogs that Ma and Pa had owned on their farm. Kindly and gently. Sing-song. And although she hadn't dared go anywhere near the vicious dogs, they'd stopped barking when they saw her approach with their food. After a few days, they'd begun to wag their tails and instead of baring their fangs, they'd wait with tongues lolling for her to throw the food within their range.

Once Annie had finished her chores, she was allowed a short time to get ready for church. Mr and Mrs Evans sat on the seat at the front of the cart while Annie travelled in the rear, her legs dangling over the back. The farmer and his wife didn't communicate on the journey. In fact, they rarely spoke, and meals were solemn occasions. Annie's entire life was now hushed – other than when she crooned to the dogs. She wasn't badly treated and once she'd been given instructions, Mrs Evans left her alone to get on with the job. It was a lonely existence.

But Ben would come soon.

A tiny worm of doubt had begun to eat away at her during the last few days. She had no idea if the Lady Amelia was still in the cove. And if it was, why hadn't Ben come yet? And then, another thought... Perhaps he couldn't find her.

Annie determined to look out for anyone she recognised and to let them know where she was so that if they should encounter Ben, they could let him know.

However, when the cart arrived outside the church, her heart leapt. There he was, leaning against a tree. She knew he'd seen her because he immediately stood straight, his body taut, but after catching her eye, he'd turned away.

Very wise.

Mr Evans, with his prim outlook, probably wouldn't allow her to talk to someone he considered a stranger so she kept her eyes down. Once Annie had accompanied Mr and Mrs Evans into the church, she didn't even know if Ben had followed or was still waiting outside.

During the service, Annie counted slowly in her head. She got as far as three thousand before she lost count and had to start again. But still, the minister pounded the pulpit and warned his errant congregation about the wages of sin. Finally, he finished. Trying to remain casually slow, Annie filed outside into the brilliant sunshine, face tilted down but eyes moving left and right, looking for Ben.

"What ails the girl? Has she lost aught?" Mr Evans asked his wife, and Annie realised she was biting her lower lip in her anguish. She immediately relaxed her mouth and continued to look meekly downwards.

The minister began to speak to Mr Evans and Annie's strange behaviour appeared to be forgotten. The conversation was brief, and Annie followed the farmer and his wife to their cart, trying to keep her face neutral while she glanced about.

Her chest grew tighter as she began to wonder whether Ben had seen her at all. Perhaps she'd been mistaken. She climbed onto the back of the cart and when Mr and Mrs Evans were settled at the front, they set off with a lurch. Annie braced herself to drop off the back of the cart. If she pretended she'd fallen, it might cause enough of a stir to attract Ben's attention.

If he was there.

Then, just as she was about to propel herself into the air, she saw him. He was crouching, hidden behind a tree by the side of the road. Her heart beat wildly in her chest. Ben had come. Relief washed through her.

But what now? She had to talk to him.

As Mr Evans set off along the track for home, it became obvious what Ben's idea was. He stepped out of the undergrowth and followed the cart at a distance. Since Annie was sitting facing the direction from which they'd come, she was able to watch him saunter along behind as if he wasn't aware of them at all. Every so often, he'd walk faster so the distance between them didn't become too great.

When Mr Evans turned into the track leading to the homestead, Annie watched Ben pass by as if he'd carried on along the road. He took off his hat as if scratching his head and she knew he was signalling to her as he'd once done when they were in the Foundling Hospital.

She suspected he'd return under cover of darkness but what of the dogs? They'd bark and alert their master unless she could get out and wait by the road.

Annie kept back some of the dogs' food when she fed them that evening. As soon as Mr and Mrs Evans retired for the night, she'd slip out and feed them the rest in the hope that they'd let her past without raising the alarm.

But what if Ben should try to approach the house before the farmer and his wife had gone to bed? Mrs Evans said goodnight at the usual hour, but Mr Evans had begun to clean his gun after supper and agonising minutes passed while he painstakingly reassembled it. Annie wondered if somehow, he knew she intended to creep out of the house and was giving her a silent warning. But that was ridiculous. He wasn't a mind-reader.

Eventually, he finished and hung his gun on the wall. After telling Annie to be up early in the morning, he finally joined his wife. Annie fetched the food she'd reserved for the dogs and after blowing out the candle, she silently let herself out of the house.

As she approached the animals, one of them began to growl and she stopped still, quietly crooning to them. His snarling turned into a whine, as he seemed to recognise her. Then he was silent, and in the darkness, she could just make out their wagging-tailed silhouettes, waiting patiently for her. Annie threw them the food and while they ate, she ran past them down the track to the road. Too late she realised she should have saved some of the food so she could return to the house without them making a sound. She could only hope they'd let her pass in silence.

Ben was there waiting, and she ran into his arms, clinging to him, her throat so constricted with emotion, she couldn't utter a sound. When he spoke, his voice too, was choked.

Finally, he said, "Annie, we have to leave."

"Leave? But how? I can't go anywhere without Mr Evan's permission."

"We have to leave Sydney. We must go now. Do you trust me?"

"Yes, of course."

"Is there anything you need to get from the house?"

"No."

"I have clothes for you to change into and then we must go." He handed her the sailor's clothes he'd found on board and told her about Towler's threat. He revealed his plan to smuggle her aboard and hide her. "I've built a false wall with a space behind for you in the wood store."

"But if I'm caught, we'll both be in trouble."

"And if you're not caught, we'll be free. Even if I stay in Sydney, I can't be with you all hours of the day. Towler means you harm and I can't bear to think of him being anywhere near you. If we make it to China, we'll jump ship and find somewhere in the world where we can be together."

A life of freedom with Ben. It was too tempting. The alternative was seven years of fear.

She stripped off in the darkness and put on the clothes Ben had given her.

With her petticoats and jacket bundled under her arm, she followed Ben along the road and down to a small, sandy cove. He'd investigated the coastline earlier and had found the beach to be the closest point of land to the Lady Amelia. It would be a long swim, but he said they'd take it slowly. Then, he'd have to smuggle her aboard without anyone spotting them.

Dark clouds moved swiftly across the sliver of moon easily blotting out its brightness. As the shore receded, the velvety blackness was relieved by pinpricks of light on the Lady Amelia ahead and a few boats close to the harbour.

After a few minutes, Ben knew Annie was tiring. She'd not recovered fully from the early stages of scurvy that had developed during the voyage and the drag of the baggy clothes he'd given her were slowing her down. But at least the trousers and jacket weren't hampering her as much as her petticoats would have done. He had an idea. Offering her his arm to hold on to while he trod water, he trapped air inside the skirts he'd been holding for her, making a float. He'd allow them time to get their breath back and then carry on.

A jolt of fear coursed through him as he heard the rhythmic splash and the creak of oar against rowlock. Annie heard it at the same instant, and she paused, silently treading water.

Longboats? No, not loud enough. There would be more than one set of oars as well as men's voices. No, this was one person rowing alone.

Someone fishing in the bay? Possibly although the boat seemed to be coming from the direction of the Lady Amelia. Blood pounded through Ben's ears as he realised it was Arthur Towler in his small rowing boat returning to town. Annie was still gripping Ben's arm. She wouldn't know it was Towler but would be alarmed that someone might find them and give them away.

As silently as he could, Ben kicked his feet and propelled them both away from the course of the rowing boat.

Splish, thud. Splish, thud. Gradually, the boat moved past them and carried on towards the shore.

The shock had given them both the strength to swim harder and within a few minutes, they'd reached the Lady Amelia. Once on board, Ben knew how to get to the carpenter's shop by the quickest, darkest route and then, he'd hide Annie away ready for the morning when the Lady Amelia would set sail for China.

An unusually large wave rocked the boat and the tools in Towler's bag moved slightly, metal clinking against metal. Towler paused, oars in mid-air, dripping...

Had anyone heard?

He listened intently. Raucous singing, music, shouting and dogs barking from the shore. The creak of the hull, slap of canvas and muffled voices from men on the main deck of the Lady Amelia. But no shouts at him to stop. Of course not. He was being foolish. But rightly so. He intended to remain a free man. As he began to dip his oars into the water once again, he heard something else. Something in the waves. Dolphins perhaps? His eyes were accustomed to the dark and he could see two shapes in the water near the hull of the Lady Amelia. Definitely not dolphins. In fact, if he didn't know better, he'd assume there were two men swimming. It was possible. Unlikely but possible that sailors had gone for a swim. He watched just to satisfy himself they hadn't noticed him. Sure enough, the figures began to climb into the ship.

The smaller one handed the larger one a bundle and then took the proffered hand. All in silence. Very strange. Towler knew when something was being done in secret. Was something being smuggled aboard? For an instant, the larger figure was silhouetted against the sail and Towler recognised him. It was that meddling fool, Haywood.

Then who was the other? As Haywood put his hand down to help the other man, Towler realised it wasn't a man at all.

It was a girl.

Haywood's convict girl.

As Towler carried on rowing to shore, a tight knot formed in his stomach. If Haywood managed to hide his girl away and thought she was safe, he'd tell Bramwell where the tools had gone. It wouldn't take the soldiers long to discover the others Towler had stolen and buried in his hut. His dream of working for himself was disappearing like smoke.

No. He wouldn't let that happen.

If the girl was discovered, she'd be returned to Sydney and punished. Serve her right. But what of Haywood? Well, he'd be punished too and who'd believe the word of someone who'd helped a convict escape? He'd be flogged and by the time anyone asked him about missing tools, they'd be halfway to China. Much too late to send the soldiers to his door. When he got home, he'd dig up the tools and find a safer place to hide them. So, even if anyone believed him, there'd be no proof.

But first, he had to ensure the girl was caught.

A trip to the tavern would do it.

A word here. A word there.

Towler knew who had scores to settle and who was keen to find favour. With any luck, there'd also be soldiers in the tavern who might easily overhear a private conversation about a female convict who was about to escape.

One way or another, Towler was confident that before the Lady Amelia sailed on the morning tide, soldiers would have been dispatched to search the ship – particularly the carpenter's shop. If that was where Haywood intended to hide her – and Towler would wager a king's ransom that it was – then it wouldn't take the soldiers long to find her.

CHAPTER 14

A red-coated captain and his soldiers boarded the Lady Amelia before first light with orders to search the entire ship. There had been a information that a female convict was hiding somewhere – possibly in the carpenter's shop.

It didn't take long to find the girl who'd been concealed behind a false wall and Mr Bramwell, ship's carpenter, was questioned. The surgeon confirmed that Mr Bramwell had been confined to bed and could have known nothing of the attempted escape. The girl refused to say who had hidden her.

One of the carpenter's men, Benjamin Haywood, came forward and confessed. The girl said she'd never seen him before but still wouldn't say who'd helped her.

Touching. But the captain was no fool. It was obvious what had happened, and Haywood was handed over to the ship's master for punishment. The girl was put in chains and taken back to Sydney to explain herself to the Governor and also to be punished by flogging.

The Lady Amelia did not sail as planned on the morning tide.

"Paperwork," the officer said. "But I'm sure everything will be in order on the morrow."

Several hours later, Mr Eli Evans, arrived at the Governor's office with an official complaint. A storm was raging over Sydney, but it hadn't deterred the dripping farmer from making his way into town to report that his convict servant had run away. Mr Evans made it clear that should the girl be found alive, he didn't want her back. He said that she'd been a sullen girl. Her work had been adequate, but he claimed that she'd interfered with his dogs, seriously upsetting them. However, he'd be obliged if a replacement for the girl could be found.

That night, Captain Yeats stepped up security on board the Lady Amelia. During the afternoon when they should have been sailing out of Port Jackson, they'd been stuck in Sydney Cove. However, the time had been put to good use by making an example of the man who'd smuggled the convict girl aboard. He'd been flogged. Twenty-five lashes. Captain Yeats knew many ship's masters who'd have insisted on more than that. Perhaps fifty or a hundred. Possibly more. But he wasn't a harsh man. He'd given the lad a chance to speak in his own defence, but he'd refused. Mr Bramwell had spoken up for him, but it was obvious the carpenter's lad was guilty. Standards had to be maintained and his crew had to understand that they must follow rules. His rules. So, that afternoon, the entire crew had watched while the bosun lashed Benjamin Haywood twenty-five times with the cat-o-nine tails.

The weather began to close in, and the captain decided to delay slightly longer before weighing anchor. Hopefully, the conditions would improve as they began to sail northwards to Canton.

In town, it was three days before the Governor was well enough to investigate the case of the runaway convict, Annie Sherrington. Both Governor Arthur Phillip and Judge Advocate David Collins had caught a fever, and both were ill. By the time they'd recovered, the ship, the Emerald, was spotted by a lookout in the signal station on the south head of the harbour. When it finally dropped anchor, it brought important letters from government ministers and a sealed package from Lord Grenville.

The matter of the escaped convict was put to one side until the urgent correspondence had been dealt with. Lord Grenville's package was opened first.

"The Duke of Westervale's granddaughter? Here?" Governor Phillips reread the letter but there was no mistake. "Find the girl immediately."

"Yes, Your Excellency."

"Prepare a room for her. She'll stay in Government House until we can arrange suitable passage home for her... Well, what are you waiting for, man? Go, go!"

Ben was half-carried to the hospital below decks where Surgeon Dawes bathed the stripes on Ben's back with vinegar and then bound him. Ben's back felt as though it was on fire.

How could he have been so reckless? It had been his idea for Annie to escape and now she'd also face punishment by flogging. She might not be so lucky as to only receive twenty-five lashes. Ben felt sick with pain and regret. And worse, Annie was still in danger of attack by Towler.

Towler! It was probably he who'd alerted the marines. Ben had heard him stop rowing the previous evening when he'd been swimming out to the ship with Annie, but didn't imagine Towler would recognise them. And now, there was nothing he could do for Annie. She was alone and vulnerable. By the time his leg irons were removed, the Lady Amelia would be at sea. He wanted to let out the screams that he'd kept inside during his flogging. He wanted to pound the cot or walls or anything else that was in range, but he knew it would achieve nothing. Instead, he lay face down, and as rage flared inside him, tears flowed into the pillow.

He'd let down the woman he loved. What use had he ever been? Even his mother hadn't wanted him.

Hopeless.

Worthless.

"Well, lad..."

Ben jumped.

Things were about to get worse. Mr Bramwell had come to see him. He gritted his teeth and waited for the abuse he was certain the carpenter would hurl at him. Had he discovered many of his tools were missing yet? *Please, no!* If he worked out that Towler had stolen them, Annie would be at risk.

Mr Bramwell cleared his throat and said again, "Well, lad... I've just come to see how you're faring."

Far from the anger Ben had expected, the carpenter sounded sympathetic.

Then, to Ben's surprise, Mr Bramwell looked up at the surgeon who was writing at his desk and while keeping his eyes on him, he pressed something small and hard into Ben's upturned palm, then curled his fingers over it to hold it in place.

"Thought you had more sense, lad." There was no ill-will in Mr Bramwell's voice. "But there it is. Done now. And you took your punishment like a man. Well, we sail tomorrow..." He looked meaningfully at Ben's leg irons and back at his curled hand. "Can't blame a man for doing what he thinks is best."

Mr Bramwell sighed, patted Ben's curled hand and stood up. He nodded at the surgeon and hobbled out of the hospital.

It wasn't until the early hours of the next morning that Ben had a chance to unlock the leg irons with the key that Mr Bramwell had slipped into his hand. The surgeon had left the hospital and when Ben saw he'd gone, he struggled to a sitting position. Each stripe opened afresh, and Ben's vision swam. He sat for a few moments, trying to push away the nausea and the darkness that slid across his vision.

It was now or never, so he had to be strong. Ben squeezed the key tightly, allowing it to bite into his palm. If he concentrated on that pain, it might take his mind off his back. It didn't, of course. But having managed to stand up, he was determined to bend down and remove the shackles.

The urge to hurry spurred him on although time took on a different meaning. Climbing familiar ladders seemed to take longer than ever before. Yet while he hid in the shadows to wait for people to pass, his way was clear before he'd noticed the people had gone and he wondered if he was fully conscious. Pain had also taken on different dimensions, but he was aware that in this strange dreamlike world where time seemed to stretch and contract, the longer he waited, the more chance there was of discovery. His aim was to get to the deck and into the choppy waves without detection, but he dared not think further than that. The lurching motion of the ship told him the waves would be enormous. It had been a challenge to swim the distance with Annie under normal conditions. But now, with such a swell... And with his back cut open and his muscles in spasm, would he even be able to keep afloat?

Ben finally made it onto the rain-lashed, wind-buffeted deck. He was instantly drenched. Soon the area would be alive with sailors, running back and forth, pulling on lines and scrambling up rigging. Or perhaps it wouldn't. Perhaps the master would wait for better weather before giving final orders to sail. In which case, it was possible – even probable that his disappearance would be discovered, and a search would follow.

Was the storm his ally or his enemy? He hoped it would keep everyone too occupied to spot his escape. Perhaps it would merely drown him.

Gripping the gunwale, he looked down into the churning waves that crashed against the hull and exploded in a foamy cloud. Two strokes of the bell rang out prompting Ben to action. He climbed onto a crate put one leg over the side, then the other and for a second or two hung on by his hands, his body dangling down the side of the ship. He screamed as his wounds broke open further and pushing himself away from the hull with his feet, he launched himself backwards. The water rose to claim him.

Gasping for breath, he broke the churning surface and tried to orientate himself. Deep in a trough, the peaks of the waves hid the land but a second later, the water raised him to the crest and he saw a few pinpoints of light in darkened Sydney. Could he be sure to keep on course? Then, to his horror, he saw triangular fins breaking the surface of the water about a hundred yards away. His back was bleeding freely and must have attracted sharks. But rather than circling him, the fins carried on past him out to sea, one breaking out of the swell as if to tell him not to be afraid. It was a dolphin. But relief was short-lived as he was sucked under a huge wave and down into the depths.

Ben struggled to the surface and tried to strike out for shore. Or at least where he thought shore lay and each time the waves hurled him upwards, he adjusted his course. Sydney didn't seem to be getting any closer. In fact, if anything, it seemed further away but still, his arms and legs pumped. His body was a knot of agony and after some time, it was as if his mind had left the pain and was hovering slightly above him. Was this what it was like to drown?

CHAPTER 15

"I don't fancy your chances, girl." The gaoler unlocked the leg irons around Annie's chafed ankles. "If you ask me, the Governor's going to make an example of you. He ain't never asked to see any escapees before. Not that we've had many who lived." He chuckled. "The last lot thought they could walk to China. Eleven of 'em left, and two returned a week later, begging us to take 'em back." He tied the bunch of keys back on his belt.

"It's hell out there in the bush. No walls but still a gaol." He scratched his chin. "No, it's worse than hell. Well, get up, girl, follow me. You don't keep Governor Phillip waiting. Not if you know what's good for you." He chuckled again. "Although it's obvious you don't know what's good for you."

Annie got unsteadily to her feet and followed the gaoler. Two soldiers had come to escort her. She was grateful that, unlike the gaoler, they kept their opinions to themselves as they marched her towards Government House and handed her over to the man who introduced himself as Thomas McKenzie, secretary to the Governor.

Mr McKenzie was tall and scholarly. He nodded at her politely and asked her to follow him. It wasn't the sort of reception Annie had expected and she wondered if he knew she was a captured escapee. He was showing such deference, he must surely think she was someone else. Even the soldiers exchanged glances before shrugging and walking away. They'd done their duty in delivering a prisoner. How the Governor's man received her was his business.

Mr McKenzie led her into a room containing a large desk and he pulled the chair into position in front of it. She was sure that when His Excellency arrived, he wouldn't be happy to see her seated, so she remained standing on the rug next to the chair. Seconds later, from another door, the man who'd spoken to the convicts on their arrival bustled into the room. He stopped and bowed politely.

"Do sit down, please, er... miss..." He hesitated over his form of address.

"Sherrington," Annie whispered. It was best to clear up who she was because sooner or later the Governor would realise he had the wrong person. Or perhaps this was how they treated people who were about to be hanged?

"Quite, quite. Miss...er Sherrington. Anne Sherrington?"

Annie nodded. "Yes, Your Excellency."

"Then, please sit, Miss Sherrington."

Annie sat down, her breath shallow and ragged. There was an undercurrent in this room that she didn't understand but it was almost certainly going to be unfavourable. She didn't want to die. Ben had gone, but he'd be back. It would take years, but she knew he'd return for her. She had seven years to serve and to wait for him. But not if they hanged her.

"So, Miss...er Sherrington." The Governor paused and looked up to the ceiling as if searching for inspiration. Then, finding none, he said, "Perhaps it is best if you read the letter yourself. It is, after all, written to you. I believe it explains the entire situation." He picked up a sheet of paper and turning it around, slid it across the desk towards her.

"You can read, I trust?"

Annie nodded and took the letter. She instantly recognised the handwriting. It belonged to Mrs Barrett. She frowned as she read the salutation, *Dear Lady Caroline.*

It was obvious now that the Governor had passed her the wrong letter. She began to slide it back to him, but he gestured for her to carry on, regarding her over the top of steepled fingers.

She read to the end of the letter. Being so closely observed by the governor was uncomfortable and she wondered if she'd been reading the words but had not taken in the meaning. She reread it. Yes, she'd definitely understood everything Mrs Barrett had written. It was nonsense, of course. Tomfoolery. Someone was making sport of her. Surely not Mrs Barrett. Then who? And to what purpose? Annie glanced at the Governor and his secretary, but neither were laughing. Not the slightest sign of mirth.

The Governor, seeing that she'd finished reading the letter, pushed two items towards her. A small, silver jewellery box and a book with a golden clasp. Annie recognised them both and drew her hands away from the two things that she'd been accused of stealing as if they might burn her. Was history repeating itself? Were they going to accuse her of stealing them again? Mrs Barrett had said in her letter they both belonged to her and that she'd been pardoned. But then she'd once believed they both had belonged to her and look how that had ended.

However, the Governor rested his chin on his steepled fingers again and nodded at her. "Take them. They're rightfully yours."

A trick? Still, Annie couldn't absorb the enormity of Mrs Barrett's words.

Finally, the Governor slid another letter across the desk towards her. "From your grandfather, the Duke of Westervale."

Annie took the letter and read the contents. Everything agreed with Mrs Barrett's account. But there had been more. He'd told her about her mother and how he wished he'd acknowledged her as his granddaughter when he'd discovered the truth about her. If he'd done that, it would have stopped Lady Constance, her great-aunt, from causing such mayhem and falsely accusing her. It was signed, dated and sealed. There could be no mistake.

Annie breathed out, having realised she'd been holding her breath. So, her mother had been the daughter of a duke who, rather than disgrace her family, had sent her to the Foundling Hospital. Hot tears slid down Annie's cheeks for her mother, for the life she might have lived, for the grandfather who'd not had the courage to own her when she'd been living as a maid in his house, for her vicious great-aunt and for the loving housekeeper who'd never given up on her. But mostly, she cried for Ben, who she yearned to tell and who, she knew, would understand how she felt, like no other person in the world.

The Duke had sent a bill of credit that would cover anything that his granddaughter required including the fare for passage home as soon as a suitable vessel docked in Sydney Cove. In the meantime, a pardon was issued, and Annie was invited to stay in Government House.

"Hopefully, passage can be arranged for you soon. I expect you're keen to get back home and to start a new life," the Governor remarked that evening at dinner. "I've no doubt your grandfather will arrange a suitable match for you."

Annie had nearly knocked over her wine glass. She was guest of honour at a dinner, the likes of which she'd have been considered too lowly to even serve in Tavistock Hall. Now, servants placed food in front of her and refilled her wine glass. And not just any servants, but convicts amongst whom, until that morning, she'd belonged.

But what had shocked her most was the idea that the Duke, the man she'd thought of as a kindly employer now had the right to arrange a marriage for her.

The Governor had only invited a few people to the dinner and had explained the circumstances, so the other guests were showing the utmost kindness. Nevertheless, Annie was nervous amongst such people who were used to having servants – not being one. Ideas chased themselves around her head and she wondered how she'd ever get used to this new life. But at the thought of returning to London and a husband, her mind froze. She would have no one but Ben. Determination shot through her.

But when she went back to London, she'd have to do as her grandfather told her.

So, don't go back to London.

Then, how would she survive? As she listened to the Governor and his guests talking, that became obvious. Sydney wasn't like London. The expectations were different here. Enterprising people – men and women – were acquiring land and then farming it. Some convicts who'd shown themselves to be trustworthy and hardworking were given land and convict servants, and they were making a success of their lives. Mr Evans and his wife were one such couple. Annie's grandfather had provided her with a large sum of money to buy new clothes and whatever she needed to keep her comfortable until she could sail back to London. The money was hers. Well, instead, she'd buy a small house and farmland where she could wait for Ben to return.

She'd send out letters with each ship that sailed into harbour hoping they'd encounter the Lady Amelia somewhere across the globe and her message would be passed to Ben so he'd know where she was. And if he arrived back in London without ever receiving one of them, then the letter she'd send to the office of the Lady Amelia's owner would be delivered to him. She knew he'd come for her.

And then, her life would begin.

The following morning at breakfast, Annie nervously put forward the idea that she might remain in Sydney for some time. The Governor frowned slightly until Annie suggested that she buy some land and have a small house built.

At that, the Governor's face broke into a smile. "A splendid idea. Yes, quite splendid."

He planned to travel to Parramatta later that morning and then on to the Hawkesbury River. Since he'd be absent for several days, he told her he'd alert Mr McKenzie to her plans and instruct him to help her with anything she needed.

Surprised that for the first time, her wishes had been taken seriously, Annie decided to suggest something else. Something more important than land and houses. And something that, if necessary, she was willing to fight for.

Taking a deep breath and bracing herself for her request to be denied, she said, "I would also like a servant." She closed her eyes, waiting for the Governor to indicate he thought she was taking liberties.

"Certainly. Mr McKenzie will arrange for it immediately."

She scanned his face to see if he was serious, but he was smiling at her agreeably over his coffee cup.

It had been as easy as that. Unbelievable.

Later, Annie went to see the secretary, and the Governor had, indeed, already briefed him.

"I have a list of convict women who are considered to be trustworthy and hardworking," he said.

"That is very kind of you, but I know who I want."

"Indeed?"

"Yes, her name is Jane Underwood, and she has two children, Samuel and Alice."

Again, she expected there to be a problem with her request, but it seemed that her new title would acquire her whatever she wanted.

"Certainly, madam. I will put that in motion immediately."

A few hours later, Mr McKenzie informed Annie that Jane Underwood and her children would arrive within the hour.

Annie waited outside Government House looking out for her friend. It was unlikely that anyone had taken the time to explain where she'd be going, and Annie expected that Jane would be worried when she was told to report to Government House. When Annie saw them walking up the hill, she ran to Jane and threw her arms around her neck.

"Oh, Jane, I have such a story to tell you!" Annie picked Sam up and swung him around, then led them to her room. She told Jane about the letters and her pardon and asked if she'd be willing to work for her.

"You'd be a servant in name only. We could work together and run the farm. The Governor says I can have some male convicts to do the hard work." Annie wondered if her change in circumstances would alter their friendship and was glad when the relief on Jane's face gave her the answer.

"But one day, you'll go home, will you not?" Jane asked with a frown.

"Perhaps. But not until Ben returns."

"I don't know much about dukes, my dear, but I suspect he wouldn't want you to marry someone like Ben."

"I'll marry Ben before we go home and then there'll be nothing anyone can do."

"*If* Ben returns..."

"Of course. I know it won't be soon. But he will come."

Jane looked down, unable to meet Annie's gaze and although she said nothing, Annie knew her experience of men told her that Ben wouldn't be back.

"If Ben is alive, he will come back to Sydney for me. That much I know," Annie said. Indeed, she'd stake her life on it.

An elderly convict, Sarah Jupp, was out searching for oysters along the shoreline in front of her hut when she came across a body lying on the beach. She crossed herself and crept closer to make sure he was dead. A sailor, by his clothes. Or possibly an escaped convict who'd dressed as a sailor. He might even have been one of those convicts who'd tried to walk to China. Only a few of them had come back. And judging by the blood on the back of his shirt, this man had met with some sort of accident. A wild beast perhaps?

Sarah poked him in the arm with the toe of her boot and leapt backwards as he groaned. His last breath? As she crouched beside him, she could see a slight rise and fall to his chest. He still lived. But not for much longer, she wagered.

Sarah hurried home as fast as she could for her husband, John. He wouldn't be happy about being disturbed from his bed, but dead bodies would mean questions and probably involve a visit from the authorities. The barrel of rum hidden in their hut might draw their attention. No, it would be best to move the dead body somewhere else. And if he wasn't dead, then a rescue might be looked on favourably by the authorities.

John Jupp pulled the grimy blanket up over his head and swore at his wife. However, Sarah continued to shake him and eventually threatened to take the barrel of rum down to the sea and tip its contents in the water. It was an empty threat. He knew she was too partial to a nip of rum to take her seriously. Sarah tried another tack, and it was the word 'reward' that finally drilled into his consciousness and brought him round.

"Who'll reward us for a corpse?" he growled.

"He ain't dead yet. But he will be afore long."

Reluctantly, John got out of bed. He put on his boots, stumbled out of their hut and down to the shore after his wife. Between them, they dragged the limp, dripping body back to their hut, and neighbours, hearing the commotion, joined them.

Sarah went through the man's pockets finding only a key which she examined carefully. It might be worth something. But other than a wooden disc tied around his neck with ribbon, there was nothing to identify him. She took that off too and it joined the key in her pocket. Being made of wood, it didn't look like it would be worth anything but might give a clue as to who he was. And of course, it might be worth something to someone if he died – which was looking increasingly likely.

"Hospital?" someone suggested, and several others nodded.

Other than groaning, the man had given no sign of coming round and the effort of having dragged him back to their house had caused fresh bleeding from his back. Sarah wasn't sure if that was a good sign or not. It was finally decided that the man definitely belonged in the hospital, and he was rolled onto a blanket. Four men took the corners and between them, the neighbours raised the man. Sarah grabbed the edge of the blanket. She'd found the man and it seemed as though things were being taken out of her hands – literally. If there was any credit due, Sarah wanted it.

While his wife was occupied, John took the opportunity to creep back to bed. Sarah and her neighbours carried the man to the hospital, and she elbowed her way to the front to explain how she'd found him, making sure the surgeon wrote down her name. When the Governor heard that she'd discovered one of the convicts who'd escaped and tried to make his way to China, then he'd know to thank her. And hopefully to reward her too.

Then remembering her basket of oysters that she'd only half-filled, she hurried home. The reward might take a while to be arranged and she and John needed something today for their bellies.

Sarah Jupp went daily to the hospital to see how 'her' man was faring. But it was disappointing. In her opinion, people hadn't taken as much interest in the case as they should have. It was clear he was one of those escapees who'd tried to walk to China. She'd been asked repeatedly why he'd been dressed as a sailor. But that was obvious too. He'd stolen the clothes. No one in their right mind would escape wearing the slops that the Governor issued to all convicts. But even so, most people considered he was a sailor who'd been washed overboard during that storm of a few days ago. Well, what did they know?

The nurses pointed to the wounds on his back. He'd been flogged recently, but there had been no floggings in the colony for a few weeks. It must have taken place on board a ship.

Hogwash. Sarah was of the opinion it had been a hitherto unknown wild beast that the escapee had encountered in the bush. But whatever had caused the wounds, several of them were infected and the man was in the grip of a fever. He raved but said nothing that made any sense. Nurses now shook their heads at his bedside and rolled their eyes at Sarah, making it clear she wasn't welcome in the hospital. She was in their way.

It was time to take action. Sarah couldn't live on rum – even if John could – and recently, she'd spent time in the hospital doing her Christian duty when she could have been on the shore gathering oysters. Once the Governor knew she'd single-handedly saved the life of a man so he could be punished for escaping, there'd be a reward. But it seemed that news of her selfless rescue had not found its way out of the hospital.

Then, Sarah would take it. From the hospital, she walked up the hill to Government House, stopping every so often to get her breath back.

"This had better be worth it," she muttered repeatedly.

When she arrived, a clerk told her that the Governor was away in Parramatta. Would she care to come back next week?

No! She would not care to come back next week. She would see someone now!

The clerk scuttled away and after a wait, she was shown in to see a tall, serious-looking man who introduced himself as Mr McKenzie. Sarah explained what she'd done and what her expectations were.

"I see, Mrs Jupp. But you say he was dressed as a sailor?"

"Yes, indeed."

"Then, what makes you think he is not a sailor?"

"It's the timing, see. It seems suspicious that men escaped and then a week or so later, one washes up. He obviously stole sailor's clothin' to make it look like he weren't a convict. He's just a clever one that's all."

"So clever, that he thought he could walk to China?"

"Well, no. Not that clever, o' course. But I knows an escapee when I sees one."

"Where have you seen escapees before, Mrs Jupp?"

Sarah tapped the side of her nose. The conversation was not going as she wanted.

Mr McKenzie sighed. "Well, it seems he's close to death, so we may never know. And if he dies, there's no way of identifying him."

"How do you know?" Her mouth fell open.

"I've had a report from the surgeon of the hospital."

So, news about the man had arrived at Government House and yet no one had contacted her. Fury surged through her. "Well, I found these on him," she said and fishing in her pocket brought out a knife, an oyster shell, a key and a wooden disc strung on ribbon. She slapped them on the desk then, after retrieving the knife and the oyster shell, she poked the other two items towards him.

Mr McKenzie picked up the key and placing it in his palm, he inspected it. "This looks as though it may have been used for handcuffs or leg irons." He turned it over. "But there's nothing on it that would help us to identify this man."

He picked up the disc by the ribbon and allowed it to swing from his fingers. "The numbers might mean something although I don't know what." He paused, frowned and looked up at the ceiling. "I believe I've seen something like this before, but I simply can't remember where. Perhaps it's some sort of identification used on one of the ships that has moored here. Well, thank you for these, Mrs Jupp. I shall investigate further."

Sarah reached out for the key and disc, but he'd already slipped them into his drawer and closed it. "Thank you for your time, Mrs Jupp." Mr McKenzie flicked the fluff and pieces of crushed shell that had come out of Sarah's pocket on the floor, then rose from his chair. The interview was over.

"But what about a reward, Mr McKenzie? I'm only asking for a little reward."

Mr McKenzie raised his eyebrows and looked down his long nose at her. "Very well. Go to the kitchen and tell Cook that Mr McKenzie sent you. She'll give you a loaf, some salt pork and perhaps some cheese if they have any."

Sarah walked down the hill back to her hut, her arms full and a smile on her face. Yes, she'd done her Christian duty. She'd single-handedly saved a man's life. The wages of sin might be death but the wages of saving a man's life were a belly full of food today and tomorrow.

"So, do I address you as Lady Caroline?" Jane's voice was light as if she was speaking in jest but there was doubt there too.

"Absolutely not! My name is Annie. I don't want there to be anything between us, Jane. I want it to be like it was when we were in prison and on the ship." Life was so surprising now, and more than ever, she needed her friend.

The women were sitting under the shade of an arbour in the Governor's Garden, watching the servants hoeing in the vegetable patch.

"This feels so wrong." Jane sighed.

"Yes, I know what you mean. A lifetime of working for others isn't easy to shake off in a day or two. My fingers are itching to do something. And I keep bracing myself for a slap or a reprimand for laziness."

Jane laughed and leaned forward towards Alice who was lying on a blanket on her back kicking her feet in the air. "Let's enjoy it while we can. It's so pleasant to just sit in the shade and draw breath—" She abruptly sat up. "Sam? Where's Sam?" She jumped up and called his name louder.

"He'll be hiding somewhere," Annie said also standing in alarm. The little boy was not used to open spaces, having been confined for most of his life. However, he was inquisitive and now, on finding he could go where he liked, where might he have wandered?

The servants in the vegetable garden stopped work and looked up at the sound of Jane's urgent shout. When she ran over to them and asked if they'd seen a little boy, one scratched his head, then shook it. Annie picked up Alice from the blanket and began a wider search. He was probably just hiding behind a tree – or even in one. She looked up but there were no convenient boughs to sit on in these grey-green trees. They'd find him shortly. He couldn't have gone far.

Jane ran back to Annie, her face white and drawn. She took Alice and held her close.

"He must be in the house," Annie said. "Perhaps he's gone back to our room. You look inside and I'll carry on searching out here."

Alice began to cry in Jane's arms as if she knew her brother was missing. Inside the building, Jane held the child close to her chest and as the sobs subsided, she heard Sam's laugh. Her skin tingled, as relief flooded through her.

She followed the sound to the door into Mr McKenzie's room. Jane groaned aloud. If Sam had caused any damage, Mr McKenzie would not be happy. How would she be able to pay for any damages? Would he recommend that Jane and her children leave this little piece of heaven in which they found themselves?

She tapped nervously on the door, swallowed and held her breath.

"Come!" Mr McKenzie called.

He didn't sound angry. Nevertheless, Sam had no idea of personal belongings since he'd only ever owned the toys that Annie's Ben and Tom, the kindly, grizzled sailor aboard the Lady Amelia, had carved for him. So, if he were let loose in an office, what damage might he do?

"Oh, no!" Her worst fears were realised.

Sam was sitting in Mr McKenzie's chair at his desk. What chaos had he caused? Then, to her surprise, she saw Mr McKenzie crouching next to him. In front of them both was an abacus.

Clack, clack, clack. Mr McKenzie slid beads across as he counted. At Jane's exclamation, Sam looked up at her, his eyes wide in astonishment and delight.

Mr McKenzie was smiling too. "Mrs Underwood your son has a remarkable gift for numbers. I'm sure he has a grand future ahead of him." He stood and patted the boy on the head, then noticing Jane's white face, his smile dropped. "I beg your pardon, Mrs Underwood, I hope you don't object to me having brought Sam in here. I saw him sitting outside on his own. He looked rather lost."

"I... I thank you, Mr McKenzie. That was most kind." She held her hand out towards the boy. "Come, Sam. Mr McKenzie is a busy gentleman."

Sam looked at her in dismay, but he slipped down off the chair.

"Thank Mr McKenzie, please, Sam."

"Thank you, sir."

Mr McKenzie's serious face broke into a smile. "Perhaps the lad could come again, Mrs Underwood. I could teach him a few letters. He certainly has an aptitude for numbers. A bright lad."

"I... I thank you, Mr McKenzie, that is most kind, most kind indeed, isn't it, Sam?"

The little boy's face lit up with joy. He couldn't resist sending one more bead across the abacus but having had to reach up to it now that he was standing, he pushed too hard and knocked it over.

Jane's heart sank. Mr McKenzie's offer had been kindly meant but he probably had no idea what it was like to spend time with a young child. She rushed forward to right the abacus.

"No need to fret, Mrs Underwood. It's a sturdy piece of equipment. I don't have children of my own." He blushed, then continued, "but I have seven younger brothers and sisters. I know that children often knock things over." He paused and stared at her. "Mrs Underwood? Is aught wrong?"

Jane was staring at the round, wooden pendant that Annie wore on a ribbon around her neck. What was it doing on Mr McKenzie's desk? Had she dropped it? She'd certainly been wearing it earlier. Sam grasped her skirts and hid his face, wondering why his mother was staring at the top of the desk.

"I believe that necklace belongs to Annie," she said.

Mr McKenzie frowned. "Do you mean the new Lady Caroline?"

"Yes, sir. This is hers... although," Jane tipped her head to one side as she stared at it. "I didn't think the ribbon was as faded as this. At least, it wasn't this morning."

"How interesting. Yes, now you come to mention it, I knew I'd seen another one. It was around Lady Caroline's neck. But this one has only just been brought to me. It was around the neck of a man who was washed up on the shore. Possibly a sailor..."

Jane pressed her hand over her mouth and stared at Mr McKenzie with large eyes.

He looked at her in alarm and indicated she should sit. "Do you know the significance of the wooden disc?"

Jane explained about Annie and Ben having been children of the Foundling Hospital and how Ben had fashioned them each one with their numbers engraved on both.

"So, there are only two of these in existence?"

"Bearing the same numbers, yes. Although I don't know if the numbers on Annie's disc are the same. But I'll wager they are."

"If the numbers are the same, then you know the identity of the man?"

"I believe so, yes. His name is Benjamin Haywood he worked for the ship's carpenter on the Lady Amelia. But you say the man was washed up. He's not—" She looked down in alarm at her son.

"Not so far, no, although I understand..." He signalled with his expression that Ben's death was likely.

"Then I must tell Annie immediately."

"Wait! For her sake, it might be prudent to be certain that the man in the hospital is Benjamin Haywood, rather than to raise her hopes unnecessarily. And of course, there is the question of his condition..."

Jane paused. Mr McKenzie was right. She needed to consider how Annie might feel.

Before she could make up her mind, from outside the room came the sound of Annie's frantic call. "Jane! Sam!"

"Oh no, poor Annie, she still thinks Sam's missing."

"Leave this to me." Mr McKenzie walked swiftly to the door and opened it. "Ah, Lady Caroline, I must apologise for having caused you and Mrs Underwood such distress. Sam has been safe with me, and we have been learning numbers. However, when I saw Mrs Underwood, I remembered that there is a slight irregularity in her paperwork which must be resolved before she can continue to work here. Nothing to be concerned about. Merely a detail. However, I was just explaining to Mrs Underwood that she must return to her overseer to obtain a signature. We were arranging that young Sam would remain with me. However, now you're here, I wonder if I could impose upon you to look after young Alice. Babies tend to become quite distraught when I get anywhere near them."

Jane drew in a sharp breath. Mr McKenzie hadn't mentioned the irregularity. She should have known things were too good to be true and then as he sent her a meaningful glance, she understood. He was giving her the opportunity to slip out to the hospital and determine whether the man was Ben. And if it was... She swallowed at the thought of how she was going to break the news to Annie if she discovered Ben had died.

Annie held out her hands to take Alice, and Jane couldn't meet her eyes. So many lies. But all to protect her friend.

Jane made her way as quickly as she could down the hill to the hospital. Mr McKenzie had scribbled a note to the surgeon to explain that Mrs Underwood was there on the Governor's business, and Jane handed it to a nurse as she entered.

As Jane approached the bed of the unknown man, he was lying on his front with his face turned away from her. It was impossible to see if it was Ben. His back was swathed in bandages and the part of his face that she could see was red and swollen. Reluctant steps took her to the other side of the bed and tears sprang to her eyes. She'd spent much of the time on board the Lady Amelia on the cramped prison deck, so she hadn't seen much of Ben, but she recognised him now.

He muttered through swollen lips, flinching and tensing in turns.

"Fever," a nurse said as she came up behind Jane. "He's burning up. Infected wounds. He was on the shore for some time before someone found him. Much longer and he'd have died... still might."

Jane gasped.

"Sorry, I thought you were one of the Governor's servants come to find out about him. I didn't realise you'd be concerned." She tilted her head to one side. "You're not Annie, are you? That's the only word he's said that's made any sense. I was beginning to think he was one of them foreigners."

"No, but I know who Annie is. She's his girl. At the moment, she doesn't know Ben is here."

"Ben, eh? Well, you might want to give some details to Surgeon White if you know who our stranger is. But in the meantime, if Annie means anything to you, I'd let her know her Ben is here. And as fast as you can. Unless his fever breaks soon, he may not be with us much longer."

Jane hurried back to Annie, rehearsing how she'd break the news and dismissing each attempt. When she got back to Government House, Annie was outside in the garden, bouncing Alice up and down. "Is everything in order now?" She frowned when Jane didn't reply immediately. "I'm sure it's just a misunderstanding. It will be sorted out... Jane? What is it?"

CHAPTER 16

Annie sat at Ben's bedside all night, her hand on his – one of the few parts of his body that wasn't bruised or cut. Even now, hours after Jane had broken the news, Annie's body was tense yet shaky. On high alert. Aware of everything and nothing. Focused on Ben's face. His eyes. His mouth. Waiting for the slightest sign that the fever would relinquish its grip. The nurse had said that he seemed calmer, but Annie wasn't sure if she was saying that to make her feel better. She hadn't noticed any improvement.

Then, as the sun began to rise, bathing Sydney Cove with shades of pink, Ben opened his eyes. For a second, he stared as if unseeing or as if seeing but not understanding what was in front of him. Annie knelt on the floor and held her face within his line of vision. Yes, something in his eyes lit up. He could see her. Then, he smiled and immediately groaned.

"Ben, my love! You've been hurt. You're in hospital. You need to rest."

Imperceptibly, he nodded, and his swollen, cracked lips parted and shaped the word, 'Yes' although no sound came out. His eyes were questioning – almost fearful.

"I'm going to stay with you."

His face softened and his eyes shone with relief.

"I'll be here. You rest."

Ben's eyelids slid shut. But the muttering and restlessness had ceased. He seemed to be peacefully asleep. The tight grip around Annie's head relaxed slightly and she allowed her shoulders to drop. The relief!

The doctor confirmed the fever had broken and it was likely that Ben would live. At last, they'd finally be together.

During the next few days, determination burned in Ben's eyes. As the angry stripes on his back faded and began to heal, he spoke to her in a rasping voice through dry, cracked lips. "Towler. Danger."

Eventually, he managed to say enough to explain that Towler had threatened Annie's life.

Shaken, she told Mr McKenzie who arranged for a red-coated soldier to accompany her to and from the hospital. Towler was also placed under surveillance. When she told, Ben he'd still seemed worried – almost disbelieving – until Annie brought the guard to his bedside.

"For you?" Ben frowned as if he couldn't believe that a soldier should be assigned to keep a convict safe.

Annie's cheeks coloured. "I've been saving my news until you're well enough." She knelt by his bed and took his hand, "It's such good news, Ben! I've received a pardon. I'm a free woman."

Ben's haggard expression softened. "Then we can go home at last?" He closed his eyes, perhaps imagining them sailing back to London.

Annie remained silent. The entire truth was a lot to take in and perhaps it was better to wait until he was completely recovered before she told him everything. After all, now he knew the authorities were keeping an eye on Towler and she was safe with a guard accompanying her, he had nothing to worry about. She was free and he could concentrate on his recovery.

As soon as he was well, their life together would begin.

The next time Annie visited, she took the letters that Mrs Barrett and her grandfather had sent explaining her origins. Ben was sitting up for the first time, with light bandages on his back. The ravages of the sun and sea were disappearing from his face and as he smiled at her, she felt those familiar fluttery feelings inside.

"This is my news." Smiling, she handed the letters to him.

He read them through and looked up at her questioning. Silently.

"Yes! I know it doesn't seem possible. I didn't believe it at first."

Ben looked down and read them again then he handed them back to her. "I'm so pleased for you. And I understand how momentous it is to learn about your mother." His tone was controlled – almost detached. But of course, it would be, it had been a lot for her to take in when she'd first read the letters and afterwards, it had taken even longer to come to terms with her new circumstances.

But once he realised how this would finally allow them to live the life they wanted, he'd be excited too.

Annie told him about the house that was being built. Their house. "The bricklayer and his men have nearly finished, and Mr McKenzie has already allocated two servants to us to start ploughing the land. By the time you're well, things will really have progressed. Oh, Ben, I can't wait for you to see it."

But her enthusiasm must have worn him out because his eyes were dark and unreadable. Not registering the eagerness she'd hoped for.

Annie asked if he was tired, and he agreed that yes, he was. So, she took her leave, reminding herself that his recovery might not be smooth. There might be great leaps and then slight setbacks. But once he was well, they'd start their life together.

However, the niggling doubt that something had changed between them gnawed at her happiness. She told herself she was being foolish.

He was simply exhausted after his ordeal, but the following day when she visited him and mentioned the progress of their house, he corrected her, "It's *your* house. Your grandfather has paid for it."

"But it will be our house when we marry."

Ben slid his hand across the bed and took hers. "Annie, we can never marry. Your grandfather will expect you to make a good match. He'd never accept me into the family." Ben shook his head sadly.

Annie's jaw dropped open. Didn't he know her better than that? "No one will match me to anyone! You and I belong together. We always have. And there's nothing my grandfather can do about it from London. I will not go back. I will stay here and marry you." She placed her hand on his, but he moved it away and shook his head.

"Annie, everything has changed. Why can't you see it? You have a wonderful future ahead of you and I can't allow you to throw it all away here on me."

Tears pricked Annie's eyes. "Have you stopped loving me?"

"No! Of course not. It's because I love you that I don't want you to give up on such a wonderful opportunity. Finally, Fate is favouring you. Don't be so quick to turn your back on everything it's offering."

It was her fault. She'd told him everything in a rush. That had been foolish. It had taken her a while to grow accustomed to her change in circumstances. It would take him time to adapt, too. They'd once shared similar beginnings; each having been given away. The only mother they'd both known had been the woman they'd called 'Ma' and they'd both been wrenched from her arms. That shared history had bound them together but perhaps now, he felt he'd lost her.

But he'd come to understand that knowing who her mother had been, was not the same as having known her. And the fact remained that they'd both been given away and had both shared their early years. Nothing could take that away, surely?

She decided to give him time to take everything. However, the following day, she sensed a change. Their oneness had gone. They might have been sitting on the opposite sides of a chasm that was slowly opening between them, dragging them apart.

Polite, formal but remote.

Surgeon White said that Ben would be well enough to leave hospital on the morrow. Annie wondered if perhaps then, he'd come and see the progress on their house. But when he spoke about leaving the hospital, he was vague about where he'd go. She'd asked the Governor and he'd agreed that Ben could stay at Government House until they were married. Ben would see how easy things would be. Yes, that was it. He simply couldn't imagine what her life was like now and where he'd fit in. But she'd show him.

Finally, she confided in Jane. Her fears spilling out along with her tears. Jane's expression was scathing. She'd never got to know Ben, but he was a man – and like all men, not to be trusted. Annie tried to convince her that he wasn't like other men, but she didn't seem convinced. However, she offered to talk to him on Annie's behalf. Surely Jane, with her common sense would persuade Ben that their life together was possible?

Jane left the children with Annie and walked down the hill. She continued past the hospital and headed towards the quay. There, she spoke to several of the sailors who were making their way to the closest tavern. She made a few enquiries about the ship that had arrived and dropped anchor in the cove a few hours before. She then hurried back to the hospital.

Ben opened his eyes when he heard her footsteps approach the bed and smiled politely when he saw her. His eyes moved past her obviously searching for Annie.

"She hasn't come. It's just me."

Ben's face, at first polite, now displayed concern. "Is Annie well?"

Jane hesitated. Was she doing the right thing? Yes. There was no other choice. Her mouth was dry, and she licked her lips trying to moisten them. "Annie will be well... when you have gone. A ship has just docked – the Cormorant. It'll set sail for India Tuesday sennight. You could be aboard. Once you're gone, Annie will be able to forget you. Then she'll truly be well."

There. She'd said it. Now, she held her breath. What would he do?

He stared at her in stunned silence. Finally, he asked, "Did Annie send you?"

"No, she thinks I came to persuade you to marry her."

"Then?"

"I value Annie's friendship and I want the best for her. She's been given a wonderful opportunity. A life of privilege. But only if you don't spoil it for her. She believes you're her future and that she loves you. But once you're gone, she'll be able to start afresh."

Ben stared at her in silence. His eyebrows drew together slightly, and a vein throbbed in his temple but otherwise, there was no reaction. Finally, he said, "I will consider your words."

"I understand you'll need somewhere to stay now you're well

enough to leave the hospital. If you decide to join the crew of the Cormorant, you'll need a little money until it sails. I know you arrived with nothing, so... here..." Jane pulled two crown coins out of her pocket and held them out to Ben.

He stared at them for several seconds. "I appreciate your offer and will take them so long as they're considered a loan." He took the coins and curled his fist around them.

"As you wish." There was nothing more to say, so Jane turned and walked out of the hospital. She didn't, however, return to Government House. Instead, she walked a short distance from the hospital and waited. Shortly after, Ben walked out into the sunshine. He paused and turning, thanked the nurses who chattered noisily and waved him off. Yes, he was indeed a handsome, young man. But there was more to a happy marriage than good looks. And Jane intended to find out what sort of man Ben was.

He walked slowly down the hill towards the quay and Jane followed at a distance. Her lip curled in disgust. So, he was going to leave on the Cormorant. Well, good riddance. It would break Annie's heart, but she was young. She'd get over it in time. And it was best to know now.

Ben needed to clear his head.

Annie wanted him to stay. To marry her. And more than anything, that's what he wanted too. But in all conscience, how could he ruin her chance at happiness?

And now, he'd been warned off by Annie's friend. She didn't think he was good enough for Annie. In fact, she was so desperate to see him go, she'd paid him off... Except she hadn't. He'd repay the money as soon as he found work. But in the meantime, he had a debt to pay.

In the harbour, there was a ship aboard which he might sail away. But where would he go? London, the town of his birth where he knew no one? Or perhaps he'd just sail the seas until he grew too old to be of any use and the sea swallowed him up.

He stood on the quayside watching the fishing boats and the longboats from the Cormorant bobbing on the waves. The salty air washed away the smell of the hospital. Vinegar, lye, herbs and the more unpleasant smells of unwashed humanity. He breathed in the fresh sea air greedily and turned his face to the warmth of the sun. His back was tender but no longer the wild fire that it had been, and his bruises had almost faded. With a little sun on his face, the marks would hardly be noticeable.

He bought a pie and some apples from a vendor and pocketed the change, then set off away from the quay along the beach. A long walk would do him good and already, his head felt clearer.

But first, there was something he had to do. He gripped the remaining crown tightly in his fist. It would take him a while to earn enough to pay Jane back but needs must.

Further along the beach, in front of a group of hovels, he saw a woman bent double, her skirts hitched up around her knees, prising something off a rock.

"Excuse me, madam, are you Mrs Jupp?"

The woman looked up, her eyes darting right and left. "Who wants to know?"

"My name is Benjamin Haywood—"

A smile broke over the woman's features. "I know who you are! Didn't I single-'andedly wrestle you from the jaws of the shark and carry you 'ome on me back?"

Ben smiled. "I came to thank you."

"Thank me?" She screwed her eyes up and looked at him suspiciously. "You came to thank me?"

"I did," said Ben, "from the bottom of my heart. I am in your debt, and I realise that this isn't a great deal but it's all I currently have to spare." He held out the crown towards her.

Doubt gave way to disbelief. Screwing up her eyes, she leaned closer, and the disbelief flickered into hope. Then, certainty lit up her face and she snatched the coin from his hand. After a rapid inspection of both sides, she tucked it into her pocket as if she thought he might change his mind. Glancing warily toward the shacks at the back of the beach, she added, "Well, that's mighty kind. Yes, mighty kind of you. I knew that you was a gent as soon as I laid eyes on you. Someone said you might be an escaped convict but I put 'em straight. 'No,' I says, 'this one's a gent.' P'raps you'd care to take a drop o' rum with me and me 'usband?" She pointed towards the ramshackle huts, then hesitated. "Only yer won't mention the crown, will yer? Mr Jupp'll 'ave it spent in no time."

He thanked her and excused himself. There were still things he had to think through, and he wanted to be alone.

Ben was out of breath and his muscles had begun to tremble after the unaccustomed exercise. He'd head back as soon as he'd recovered his breath. There was still a hill to climb.

He sat down on a rock and watched Mrs Jupp waddle back to one of the huts. She disappeared inside and emerged a few moments later without her basket and fastened a bonnet on her head. With a glance backwards to the interior of the hut, she closed the door and set off towards town.

When she was out of sight, Ben turned so he was looking out to sea. Clouds drifted across the sun, muting the harsh brilliance of the light that glinted off the waves. It was calm today with no hint of the fury that had been unleashed the night he'd almost drowned.

But he hadn't drowned. Fate had dragged him from the depths and brought him up on this shore for the woman who lived in the hut behind him to find. And he might yet have died of his infected wounds.

But he hadn't. Didn't that mean something? He'd been given a second chance with Annie. She'd made it clear she still wanted him until he'd foolishly rejected her. Yes, he'd had her welfare at heart but in truth, hadn't he been afraid? He couldn't compete with dukes and earls. Neither could he compete with what they'd be able to offer her. But when had Annie ever demanded anything? Of course, everything could have changed when she'd discovered she was part of the Farringdon family. However, she'd made it clear that she wanted a life with him. So, was it too late? He watched the waves drag pebbles down the beach as they retreated. His thoughts were like those pebbles, as doubt washed over them, rolling them over and bearing them away.

He was sure of Annie.

And yet, her friend had bribed him to go away.

Had Annie put her up to it?

No, he wouldn't allow himself to believe that of Annie. She wasn't deceitful. She'd have told him to his face.

Over and over, his thoughts tumbled.

He pulled the wooden token from inside his shirt and grasped it tightly in his fist, hoping for an answer. Annie had brought it to him while he was in hospital, and he'd seen that she still wore hers.

Why would she have worn it if she didn't want any part of him?

In truth, he didn't know.

Then ask me. Annie's voice said from within the confusion of his thoughts.

That was it. He needed to hear what Annie wanted from her own lips. He stood up and set off along the beach on unsteady legs. It felt as though he'd been walking for weeks but Annie's face was foremost in his mind, and it was as if that invisible cord that bound them together was pulling him up the hill. He held on tightly to the wooden token, trying to draw strength from that. His number, and Annie's number. Back-to-back.

Side-by-side. As one. If that was what she wanted.

When he arrived at Government House, the babble of voices and music spilled out into the afternoon sunshine. The Governor had guests. Ben stopped. Now what? He could hardly knock at the main door dressed in the clothes the hospital had provided for him, with bruises on his face, and then ask for Lady Caroline. No, he'd have to go to the servants' entrance. But if the Governor had guests, then she wouldn't want to be disturbed. And if she did come to see him, Ben didn't want to embarrass her with his shabby appearance in front of the servants.

But the Annie of old wouldn't care what he looked like. If she was still the same person.

If.

He summoned his courage and knocked.

Jane opened the door, her arms full of blankets and cushions. She peered over the top, expecting to see a servant of one of the Governor's guests, so when she saw Ben, she grunted in surprise.

What could he want? His conscience had prompted him to say farewell to Annie, she supposed. Oh well, at least he'd had the decency to do that. She'd assumed he'd spend his time – and her money – in the taverns until he was aboard the Cormorant and then sail out of Annie's life forever. Not that it would help Annie at all that he'd come. It'd simply draw out the pain. But at least she'd hear it from his lips rather than from Jane's.

She'd dreaded telling her friend that her mission to persuade Ben to remain had failed. Of course, she hadn't gone into details about her methods, but the result was the same. If she'd begged him to stay for Annie, he may well have done. Instead, she'd offered him an easy way out. She'd goaded and bribed him. If he'd been true, he'd have sent her away. But he hadn't. He'd taken her money and had gone straight to the quay to find employment on the Cormorant.

Not, of course, that she'd actually seen him talk to anyone on the wharf, but it wasn't a place that she'd been keen to return to. It'd been bad enough having been down there earlier to find out about the Cormorant. Not only had the sailors been insufferable but the women who'd loitered there had told her to be off and leave the custom to them. They were welcome to it. But why else would Ben have gone to the quay?

And now, here he was.

"She's not here," Jane said with some satisfaction.

Ben's face fell.

For a second, Jane's resolve wavered. He looked quite ill. Well, she didn't want to see him suffer. "You'd better come in. I'll fetch you some refreshment."

"Thank you but I wouldn't want to embarrass Annie. I just wanted to see her."

Jane sighed. "When I told her you'd be leaving on the Cormorant, she couldn't face seeing anyone."

Ben spluttered, "Why did you tell her that?"

"Because I followed you to the quay and guessed why you'd gone there—"

"But I'm not leaving!"

"Then why did you go straight to where you'd find employment?"

"It's none of your business but I didn't go to the quay—"

Jane snorted in derision. "Liar! I followed you."

"I bought some food and then I carried on past the quay to the beach. I wanted to thank the woman who saved my life." He took the remaining coins from his pocket and held them out to her. I will pay back the rest. You have my word."

"Oh!" Jane looked at him in horror. "Then, you do want to be with Annie?"

"More than ever and more than anything."

Jane hesitated. He was a man and she'd suffered at the hands of various men. And yet... Annie had placed her trust in this particular man. Recently, Jane had seen that not all men were unreliable. Mr McKenzie had shown her and the children the utmost kindness.

She stared into Ben's eyes. Had she jumped to conclusions about his intentions at the wharf? What she saw there suggested that yes, it seemed she had misjudged him. She clenched her fists and bit her lip. He might still be lying. How could she be sure of his intentions?

She couldn't.

So, didn't Annie deserve the opportunity to make up her own mind? Yes, it was up to Annie. Jane knew exactly what she was going to do. "Wait there. Do not move. I'll put this right."

She ran to find Mr McKenzie, amazed at how she'd come to rely on his good sense and kindness.

"You're sure of the man's good intentions?" he said when she explained how she'd gone to the hospital and tested Ben and how he was now there, looking for Annie.

Jane hesitated. "Well, I'm as sure as I can be."

"Then I'd say your idea is sound. The cart is ready by the stables, and I'll tell the driver he'll be taking one man. Such a shame. I know Sam was looking forward to it but perhaps I can distract him? I promised to show him how to play chess. I could show him tonight?" Mr McKenzie's serious face lit up. "And perhaps you and Alice would join us? I'd deem it a great honour."

Jane nodded. There was something about this man that filled her with warmth and comfort. She wanted nothing better than to spend the evening with him. And that would give Annie and Ben a chance to talk.

CHAPTER 17

Annie swept the sawdust into a pile. She'd probably missed some. It was hard to see through her tears. Wiping her eyes on her sleeve, she set to again with vigorous brush strokes. Jane and the children would be with her soon and she wanted it to be as clean as possible after the day's work.

Poor Jane. It had been hard delivering such bad news. Annie hadn't believed it could be true. There was a misunderstanding. Surely? She'd run down to the hospital, but Ben had already left and one of the nurses confirmed that he had, indeed, walked in the direction of the wharf.

She'd slowly returned to Government House, having forgotten that Governor Phillips was entertaining several of the military officers and their wives. Jane suggested she go to her house. Not that it would take her mind off Ben. It was where, in her dreams, she'd seen them both. But at least the workmen wouldn't take any notice of her and once they'd gone, she'd be alone. Jane said she'd join her later and bring the children. Perhaps they could stay the night? Annie had agreed.

It had been a kind thought but Annie had always imagined her first night in the house would be with Ben. Now, nothing would ever be with Ben again.

She hurled the broom away and sitting on the floor, she gave herself up to sorrow, disappointment and anger. Hot tears stung her eyes and as the pain welled up inside, she threw her head back and roared like a wounded animal. She hadn't asked to be a duke's granddaughter. She hadn't asked to be given away by her mother and then hidden away in shame by her grandfather. All she'd asked for was Ben. He was all she wanted. And now, because of the family who'd betrayed her, he'd gone.

She looked around the bare room. The roof had been finished today but the windows and doors were just holes in the walls. She'd imagined how it would look when she and Ben lived there but now, she saw it as it was. Hollow and empty. Much like her. Well, she'd never live here. Not on her own.

Then, where would she go? She didn't belong anywhere. Had her entire life been a meaningless waste of time?

The jingle of a horse's harness brought her back to the present. Jane had arrived with the cushions, blankets and food that they'd enjoy that night. *Enjoy.* She didn't think she'd ever enjoy anything again. Well, she'd pretend. Perhaps that was what the future held. Pretence.

She stood and cleared up the pile of sawdust, all the while, practising a smile. There waso need to make others miserable. Simply pretend all was well.

Yes. She could do that.

Footsteps approached and Annie turned to the empty doorway. The cart driver, with arms full of bedding and a basket of food, cleared his throat politely to announce his arrival. Annie fixed the new polite smile on her face and gestured for the man to place them in the middle of the floor. As he left, she arranged the bed rolls for her and Jane with a space between them for the children. How excited Sam would be at the prospect of sleeping somewhere different. She must ensure they all enjoyed it. *Pretence. That's the answer. Simply pretend.*

When she was satisfied, she looked up, expecting the driver to reappear with the children's bedding but she could only see his shadow outside the door. What was he waiting for? Then, she heard the driver click his tongue as he flicked the reins, followed by the trundle of wheels and clop of hoofs. She rushed to the door to stop him before he carried the children's bedding back. And anyway, where were Jane and the children?

Annie ran outside in time to see the rear of the cart as it turned onto the track back to Government House. So, who was waiting outside casting a shadow across her door?

She froze as she saw him. "Ben?" Her voice was barely audible.

"Annie."

But he didn't rush to her and gather her up in his arms as he once would have. He'd never been ill-at-ease with her before. But then, he'd never voluntarily left her before.

So, he'd come to say farewell. She knew he was a good man and that he'd never have simply walked away. Would it have been better for her if he had? Either way was unbearable. She felt the tug of the invisible cord that bound them and knew that it would be the last time. Today, it would be severed and they'd both drift away from each other like ships carried on different tides.

Annie swallowed down the bitter taste in her throat. "If you've come to bid me farewell, please say it and go." Her voice was harsher than she'd intended but the lump in her throat had squeezed all feeling from her words.

"Is that what you want? For me to say goodbye?"

He had the audacity to sound hurt!

"What does it matter what I want? Jane said you're leaving on the Cormorant. So, why don't you just go?" Her throat tightened further. If he didn't leave soon, she wouldn't be able to speak at all. She turned away. He'd fulfilled his duty. Now let him leave or she'd break down.

"Annie! No! Jane was wrong. I'm not leaving. I can't live without you, and I came to see if you still wanted to be with me. But... But perhaps I'm too late..." Ben half-turned to go.

"Wait!" Had she misheard? "You say you're not leaving?"

"Not unless you want me to go."

"How can you ask that? You know I want you to stay."

"Then?" He opened his arms and Annie ran to him and threw her arms around his neck.

They clung together, silently. There was no need for words.

"Come," she finally whispered and taking his hand, she led him into the house.

Now Annie realised why the driver hadn't brought bedding for the children. Jane didn't intend to come. Instead, she'd sent Ben to her.

Annie led him through the house, willing him to become engaged with it and not to simply stand back as though he had no part of the place. Without him, it would just be bricks and wood. But he immediately took an interest in the craftsmanship and began to point out things that needed to be done, suggesting ways of doing them.

"You'll need windows and doors in as soon as possible."

"No." She shook her head and placed her finger over his mouth. "*I* won't need windows and doors. *We* will need windows and doors. And I'm relying on you to do them."

He playfully nipped her finger and smiled. "I shall start now."

"You'll do no such thing. Your back is only just healed and anyway, we have food to eat and plenty to catch up on. I want to know what happened after I left the Lady Amelia."

They sat outside on a blanket on what would one day be their veranda and ate their meal watching the sky turn crimson as the sun set.

"Will they send someone for you to take you back to Government House or will you walk?" Ben asked.

"No, I intended to stay here tonight."

"But you can't stay on your own."

"Indeed, I can't. But I won't be on my own because you'll be here." She took his hand. "You will be here, won't you?"

He smiled at her. "You just want to make sure your carpenter starts early in the morning!"

Relief washed away all anxiety. They were together. Ben was already making plans for their house. They were teasing and laughing as they'd always done.

Well, perhaps not all anxiety had gone. This was the first night they'd ever spent alone together.

A colourful blurred streak of lorikeets flew past and alighted in a tree some way off, chattering and whistling excitedly. Ben sighed.

"I'm beginning to like this country. It's harsh but it has a raw beauty. When I think of London now, my memories are coloured grey and brown. But here, things are so much brighter. So much more intense."

"Well, let's enjoy it. Neither of us has any reason to go back. And think of all the 'firsts' we'll have here. You know, this has been the first meal we've ever eaten alone together. In our first home."

Ben put his arm around her shoulders. "D'you realise, this is the first time we've ever been able to relax alone in each other's company since we were infants. When we used to meet through the laundry window in the Foundling Hospital, I kept looking over my shoulder, starting at every sound. I'm sure the cats knew how frightened I was. They used to creep up and rub against my legs. I can still recall how scared I was."

Annie laughed. "I don't know how I didn't break my neck balancing on that bench trying to reach out the window to touch your fingers. And even when we hid away on the ship, we were never more than a few yards from someone. But here in Sydney, it's like we can be ourselves." Annie snuggled against him and placed her hand on his shoulder. "Now, what other firsts can we achieve this evening?" She slowly moved her hand down over the contours of his chest.

"Annie!" He groaned as he playfully trapped her hand beneath his. "Do you realise what you're doing to me? I may work with wood but I'm not made of it."

She wriggled her finger between two buttons, inside his shirt and stroked his skin.

"Annie! Please stop. We'll marry as soon as we can and then—"

She lay back on the blanket, then pulled him down beside her. Flicking one button undone and then another, she slipped her hand inside and lay the palm over his heart. It beat a frantic tattoo. Like hers. "Let's not wait any longer. We've always belonged to each other. Like God made us for each other. A service in a church will only tell others what we already know." She opened another button and leaning over him, she placed her lips against the smooth, thrumming skin over his heart. His scent filled her nostrils, and she closed her eyes, listening to his heartbeat. Or was it the blood pounding through her ears?

Annie sat up and reaching behind, she began to undo her stays. Ben took the laces from her hands and slowly unlaced her, nuzzling her neck until the garment slipped off. Then, as the sun sank below the horizon, he revealed each part of her body, and she trembled as his lips glided over her skin.

CHAPTER 18

1793:

Three babies. Side-by-side in their mothers' arms. A girl and a boy, held by their mother, Mrs Annie Haywood. And another girl in the arms of her mother, Mrs Jane McKenzie. And behind, stood the proud fathers. Benjamin Haywood, and Thomas McKenzie holding the hands of his stepchildren, Sam and Alice.

The baptism service in the church was well attended. After all, everyone knew that Annie was the granddaughter of a duke. They also knew that Mrs McKenzie was still officially a convict, but her husband was a trusted member of the new Governor's staff. An important man.

Annie and Ben were keen that the twins' aristocratic connections were forgotten. No easy task when local farmer, Eli Evans told anyone who'd listen that Annie had briefly stayed on his farm, conveniently forgetting that she'd slept in the kitchen and had been constantly scolded for not working fast enough.

"I knew she were special. I could tell immediately that she weren't a common convict. She 'ad such a way with my dogs too. But them nobility know all about 'orses and dogs, don't they?"

Annie looked back from the sea of faces of the people who'd gathered for the baptism to the children nestled in her arms. Angelic faces. Eyes closed and peaceful expressions. She smiled when she remembered how outraged they'd been when Reverend Parker had held them. Their screams had woken up placid, baby Elizabeth who'd joined in from Jane's arms. The twins' heads were covered in silky, dark copper hair. Not as dark as Ben's nor is fiery red as hers. And yet they seemed to have inherited her temper.

Well, the temper she'd once had. Her fire had burnt low over the years but not quite burnt out. Hopefully, these children would never be worn down in a similar way. While she had breath in her body, she'd ensure that was so. Annie's throat tightened. Were there ever any children as loved as these? They'd never need to wonder where they'd come from and why they'd been rejected. These children would know they were wanted. Adored. Annie met Ben's gaze and understood they were sharing the same thoughts.

She knew that over the years, Ben had coped with his past by ignoring it and she'd wondered if he'd agree to them naming the children after the people they'd believed to be their parents. Thankfully, Ben had liked the idea and now Isabella and James had been christened with names that no one would ever take away from them and replace with others.

One day, when the twins were old enough to understand, Annie would tell them about Ma and Pa, their namesakes.

She'd written to Trent Farm in Essex to tell them about her and Ben and their two children. It was unlikely Isabella and James would ever meet Ma and Pa. But perhaps they'd meet up with Robbie and Sarah, one day.

Ben put his arm around her and leaned his head against hers. It was as if all the guests had faded away.

They were together.

Annie and Ben with their children. Side-by-side. They were as one.

***

Please consider leaving a review for this book on Amazon and Goodreads, thank you.

About the Author

Dawn spent much of her childhood making up stories filled with romance, drama and excitement. She loved fairy tales, although if she cast herself as a character, she'd more likely have played the part of the Court Jester than the Princess. She didn't recognise it at the time, but she was searching for the emotional depth in the stories she read. It wasn't enough to be told the Prince loved the Princess, she wanted to know how he felt and to see him declare his love. She wanted to see the wedding. And so, she'd furnish her stories with those details.

Nowadays, she hopes to write books that will engage readers' passions. From poignant stories set during the First World War to the zany antics of the inhabitants of the fictitious town of Basilwade; and from historical romances, to the fantasy adventures of a group of anthropomorphic animals led by a chicken with delusions of grandeur, she explores the richness and depth of human emotion.

A book by Dawn will offer laughter or tears – or anything in between, but if she touches your soul, she'll consider her job well done.

If you'd like to keep in touch, please sign up to her newsletter on her blog and receive a welcome gift, containing an exclusive prequel to The Duchess of Sydney, three short humorous stories and two photo-stories from the Great War.

You can follow her here on https://dawnknox.com
Amazon Author Central: mybook.to/DawnKnox
on Facebook: https://www.facebook.com/DawnKnoxWriter
on Twitter: https://twitter.com/SunriseCalls
on Instagram: https://www.instagram.com/sunrisecalls/
on YouTube: shorturl.at/luDNQ

The Duchess of Sydney
The Lady Amelia Saga – Book One

Betrayed by her family and convicted of a crime she did not commit, Georgiana is sent halfway around the world to the penal colony of Sydney, New South Wales. Aboard the transport ship, the Lady Amelia, Lieutenant Francis Brooks, the ship's agent becomes her protector, taking her as his "sea-wife" – not because he has any interest in her but because he has been tasked with the duty.

Despite their mutual distrust, the attraction between them grows. But life has not played fair with Georgiana. She is bound by family secrets and lies. Will she ever be free again – free to be herself and free to love?

Order from Amazon: mybook.to/TheDuchessOfSydney
Paperback: ISBN: 9798814373588
eBook: ASIN: B09Z8LN4G9

The Finding of Eden
The Lady Amelia Saga – Book Two

1782 – the final year of the Bonner family's good fortune. Eva, the eldest child of a respectable London watchmaker becomes guardian to her sister, Keziah, and brother, Henry. Barely more than a child herself, she tries to steer a course through a side of London she hadn't known existed. But her attempts are not enough to keep the family together and she is wrongfully accused of a crime she didn't commit and transported to the penal colony of Sydney, New South Wales on the Lady Amelia.

Treated as a virtual slave, she loses hope. Little wonder that when she meets Adam Trevelyan, a fellow convict, she refuses to believe they can find love.

Order from Amazon: https://mybook.to/TheFindingOfEden
Paperback: ISBN 979-8832880396
eBook: ASIN B0B2WFD279

The Other Place
The Lady Amelia Saga – Book Three

1790 – the year Keziah Bonner and her younger brother, Henry, exchange one nightmare for another. If only she'd listened to her elder sister, Eva, the Bonner children might well have remained together. But headstrong Keziah had ignored her sister's pleas and that had resulted in Eva being transported to the far side of the world for a crime she hadn't committed. Keziah and Henry had been sent to a London workhouse where they'd been separated but when the prospect of work and a home in the countryside is on offer, both Keziah and Henry leap at the chance.

But the promised job in the cotton mill is relentless, backbreaking work and Keziah is full of regret that her wilfulness has led to such a downturn in her family's fortune.

Then, when it seems she may have discovered a way to escape the drudgery, the charismatic but irresponsible nephew of the mill owner shows his interest in Keziah. But Matthew Gregory's attempts to demonstrate his feelings – however well-intentioned – invariably result in trouble for Keziah. Is Matthew yet another of Keziah's poor choices or will he be a major triumph?

Order from Amazon: https://mybook.to/TheOtherPlace
Paperback: ISBN 979-8839521766
eBook: ASIN B0B5VPLHGQ

The Dolphin's Kiss
The Lady Amelia Saga – Book Four

Born 1790; in Sydney, New South Wales, to wealthy parents, Abigail Moran is attractive and intelligent, and other than a birthmark on her hand that her mother loathes, she has everything she could desire. Soon, she'll marry handsome, witty, Hugh Hanville. Abigail's life is perfect. Or is it?

A chance meeting with a shopgirl, Lottie Jackson, sets in motion a chain of events that finds Abigail in the remote reaches of the Hawkesbury River with sea captain, Christopher Randall. He has inadvertently stumbled across the secret that binds Abigail and Lottie. Will he be able to help Abigail come to terms with the secret or will Fate keep them apart?

Order from Amazon: https://mybook.to/TheDolphinsKiss
Paperback: ISBN: 979-8842582969
eBook: ASIN: B0B85JX9BD

THE PEARL OF APHRODITE
The Lady Amelia Saga – Book Five

In 1790, three-year-old Charlotte Jackson is transported with her convict mother from London to Sydney. Twenty-one years later, Charlotte is offered the chance of a new life in London by the mysterious and brash Ruth Bellamy. Charlotte yearns to belong. A new start in a new country might be just what she needs.

On the perilous voyage, she falls for handsome Alexander Melford, also seeking betterment in London.
Fate throws them together. But the deceit of those they trust threatens to tear them apart. Will they ever escape the lies and finally be free to love?

Order from Amazon: https://mybook.to/ThePearlOfAphrodite
Paperback: ISBN: 979-8356843648
eBook: ASIN: B0BKSPC93Z

Other works by Dawn Knox

The Great War
100 Stories of 100 Words Honouring Those Who Lived And Died 100 Years Ago

One hundred short stories of ordinary men and women caught up in the extraordinary events of the Great War – a time of bloodshed, horror and heartache. One hundred stories, each told in exactly one hundred words, written one hundred years after they might have taken place. Life between the years of 1914 and 1918 presented a challenge for those fighting on the Front, as well as for those who were left at home— regardless of where that home might have been. These stories are an attempt to glimpse into the world of everyday people who were dealing with tragedies and life-changing events on such a scale that it was unprecedented in human history. In many of the stories, there is no mention of nationality, in a deliberate attempt to blur the lines between winners and losers, and to focus on the shared tragedies. This is a tribute to those who endured the Great War and its legacy, as well as a wish that future generations will forge such strong links of friendship that mankind will never again embark on such a destructive journey and will commit to peace between all nations.

"This is a book which everyone should read - the pure emotion which is portrayed in each and every story brings the whole of their experiences - whether at the front or at home - incredibly to life. Some stories moved me to tears with their simplicity, faith and sheer human endeavour." (Amazon)

Order from Amazon: mybook.to/TheGreatWar100
Paperback: ISBN 978-1532961595
eBook: ASIN B01FFRN7FW
Hardcover: ISBN 979-8413029800

THE FUTURE BROKERS
Written as DN Knox with Colin Payn

It's 2050 and George Williams considers himself a lucky man. It's a year since he—like millions of others—was forced out of his job by Artificial Intelligence. And a year since his near-fatal accident. But now, George's prospects are on the way up. With a state-of-the-art prosthetic arm and his sight restored, he's head-hunted to join a secret Government department—George cannot believe his luck.

He is right not to believe it. George's attraction to his beautiful boss, Serena, falters when he discovers her role in his sudden good fortune, and her intention to exploit the newly-acquired abilities he'd feared were the start of a mental breakdown.

But, it turns out both George and Serena are being twitched by a greater puppet master and ultimately, they must decide whose side they're on—those who want to combat Climate-Armageddon or the powerful leaders of the human race.

Order from Amazon: mybook.to/TheFutureBrokers
Paperback: ISBN 979-8723077676
eBook: ASIN B08Z9QYH5F

Printed in Great Britain
by Amazon

39451230R00079